Knotty Works

an erotic retrospective

NightEyes DaySpring

Dancing Jackal Books

Knotty Works: an erotic retrospective

First Edition Paperback, 2022

ISBN 978-1-957364-02-5

Dancing Jackal Books
Tallahassee, FL
www.dancingjackalbooks.com

Cover illustrated by Erkhyan Rafosa – *twitter.com/Erkhyan*

Dedicated to all the beta readers I've worked with over the years whose insights have helped shaped the stories in this book.

Contents

Foreword

The tales in this book have been written over the better part of a decade. While they all deal with the sexual aspect of gay relationships in some way, that doesn't mean there's not a lot of story in these stories. From the 1950s to 40,000 feet above the Atlantic, the twelve stories in this collection explore love, life, and the serious aspects of living.

The oldest story in here dates from 2014, while the newest story I wrote last year, and I've left a brief note before each story to let you know where it comes from and what to expect. Everything in this book has been previously released, but they're scattered across different anthologies and my Patreon. While this doesn't have all the adult writing I've put out in the last decade, it does cover a good swath of it. It also brings together stories that have sequels in one book.

I hope you enjoy the selections I've included.

NightEyes DaySpring, February 2022

Foxing for Pizza appeared on my Patreon in 2020 and has more meat related jokes than anything I have ever written. But then, sometimes what you want is a good slice and some "sausage" to go with it. It also very much uses the word fox as a verb. This story also has a wonderful reading done by Khaki for The Voice of Dog *podcast.*

Foxing for Pizza

When he said he wanted pepperoni and sausage on his pizza, Alex knew he was going to be getting meat, but he didn't know he was going to have to take some meat to get his pizza. It wasn't like he hadn't taken a dick for DiGiorno before, but he thought tonight he might get away with just licking some sausage. Leo though, had different ideas.

"God, you're tight," grunted the black-backed jackal.

The fox wiggled his hips, feeling the shaft inside of him shift around. "We should do this more often then and loosen me up."

The jackal barked, amused, and gripped the fox's hips. "Well, you said you wanted sausage tonight and I'm going to give it to you." He shoved himself all the way into the fox, pushing his knot against him, filling him.

"Yeah!" he yipped. "Give me all your meat. Fill me with your cheesy goodness."

Suddenly he felt his whole body shaking like an earthquake. "Hey, hey, wake up man!"

℔

"Wha?" mumbled Alex, blinking at the jackal standing over him. He was on the couch, the video game controller still clutched in one paw.

"Man, you mumble some fucked up shit when you are asleep," said Leo. "'Fill me with your cheesy goodness?' What the fuck is that?"

"Oh uh, nothing. Just dreaming about food." The image of Leo being deep inside of him came back to him. "Uh. Nothing at all."

The jackal plopped down in the chair next to the couch, clutching a can of soda. "Yeah, yeah. I heard something about sausage also."

The fox sat up and pulled his shirt to straighten it, realizing then he had a hard-on showing through his boxers. He tried to flick his tail to cover it up, but it was pinned under his leg. The jackal just shook his head watching this.

"That looks like one of your dreams again."

"Hey, there is nothing wrong with having an overactive imagination, if it gets you laid in your sleep."

Leo just shrugged and pulled out his phone. "I just dream about stupid shit: studying for school, washing the dishes, and being stuck at work. It tends to be pretty mundane."

"I can't help it if it my mind gets creative for me. It's good to have fantasies."

"Yeah, yeah. You tell me that all the time. Hey, you want to get some dinner or are you ready to turn in for the night?"

The fox considered for a moment and then smiled. "I could eat."

"You know what you want?"

His imagination had told him exactly what he was craving, and his stomach made a growling sound to reinforce it. "Pizza, but we don't have any frozen pizza left."

Leo tapped his phone. "We can always get some delivery."

He frowned. "I'm kind of broke right now. I don't get paid till Friday. I had to pay my car insurance for the next six months yesterday. I guess it will be ramen again tonight."

The jackal made a gagging sound. "That stuff is either too salty or it doesn't have any taste."

"So, don't add the whole flavor packet," Alex shifted around so he could stop sitting on his tail. "The good old college standby never fails."

"You know I think that cheap stuff is nasty." Leo shuddered. "Pizza does really sound good though," he added, pulling up a local place on his phone. "Maybe Hawaiian."

"Oh, come on. You know I don't like pineapple on pizza."

The jackal chuckled. "You said you couldn't afford it."

"Yeah, but I was just dreaming of splitting a pizza with you." Okay, he'd been dreaming of a lot more than pizza, but the jackal didn't need to know that. "I would be happy to pay you back."

"Uh huh. What was that you were mumbling about before I woke you up? Oh right, something about being filled with cheese or something."

The fox's ears lowered. "Okay, so it wasn't *just* pizza I was dreaming about."

"Oh really?" he said, leaning forward, ears focusing on Alex. Leo put his drink down on the end table and his tail thumped against the chair. "Why don't you tell me."

"Uh… well there was sausage."

"Uh huh."

"Sausage in me…"

"You dreamed about being fucked by a piece of sausage?"

"No! I mean yes, but it was your sausage," the jackal gave him a surprised look, "and hey… it was a dream, okay? Mine get a little weird sometimes."

Leo put his phone down. "What am I, just a piece of meat to you?"

His ears splayed. "Hey, you are way more than just a piece of meat to me. You're my friend, my housemate…" *and sexy too*, but now wasn't the time for Alex to mention that.

"Uh huh. According to your subconscious, I'm just a piece of meat for you to enjoy."

The fox rolled his eyes. "Like you complained last time. I seem to recall you were quite happy for me to share my sausage with you."

"One time. I take it one time, and you won't let me live it down."

"Well maybe," said the fox, stretching back on the couch, "I should share mine with you more often."

"Yeah, maybe not," said the jackal, picking up his phone. "We're housemates, not lifemates. Anyway, what type of pizza do you want?"

Alex pouted. "You are no fun, and I'm still broke."

The jackal shrugged. "No meat for you then."

The fox whined. "But I'm hungry."

"Uh huh," Leo just tapped on his phone.

Alex rolled off the couch onto the floor and crawled over to the chair on all fours. His tail wagged in anticipation. "Perhaps we can make a deal."

"I'm getting Hawaiian."

The fox crept up the chair a little so he could look up at the jackal from about waist height. "What would it take for you to order something with sausage on it?" His tail wagged slowly.

Leo looked down at him. "And what are you offering?"

"Well, I'm hungry, and I'd do anything for some meat I enjoy. Ramen is nice, but I don't have the stuff to make good ramen."

The jackal reached down to tickle the underside of the fox's muzzle. "Anything?"

Alex smiled. "Within reason of course, but you won't complain." A paw reached up and gently tugged at the zipper of the jackal's shorts. "You aren't going to order Hawaiian now, are you?"

"Still thinking about it."

He leaned over and sniffed around the jackal's crotch with his nose. "Think a little harder."

Leo smirked. "Hey, I do like pineapple."

The fox undid the button of the jackal's shorts and pulled them back. "Well, I've got my heart set on sausage." He tugged down the hem of the boxers Alex wore and kissed the pink tip peeking out of the jackal's sheath. "I think you do too."

Leo shifted his hips. "I can be convinced," he said, tapping on his phone, as the fox nuzzled his sheath, drawing out his shaft. Slowly it hardened as the warm breath from the fox's muzzle washed over him. Finally, Alex clicked order on the pizza and tossed the phone on the couch as his shaft was coming to full attention. "It should be here in twenty to thirty minutes, and since I ordered the works, why don't you show me the works."

"Sausage and pepperoni together with vegetables? You do spoil me!"

The jackal nodded.

A tongue licked up the jackal's shaft. "I'll have to do something special for you then."

Leo leaned back in the chair, pressing his crotch forward toward the fox. "Then you better get busy."

The fox chuckled and reached to take the base of the jackal's penis, licking up the member slowly, savoring the feeling of it on his tongue. The jackal's arousal gave off a strong, familiar musk. Since he'd moved in with Leo, the scent was always present in the apartment, but during sex it was stronger, sharper. Alex knew his own scent responded in kind.

He took his time with the shaft, making sure to get it nice and wet, feeling it gently throb at his touch, not wanting to push the jackal too far too quickly. He wanted to earn his treat, and his own maleness had slipped free of his sheath and was now peeking out of his boxers. He shifted his weight, listening to the increasingly ragged breathing of the jackal.

"You'll play with that all day if I let you," said Leo with a pant.

The fox flicked his ears back and closed his eyes, drawing his tongue up slowly in response. The jackal squirmed under him.

"Is that the only way you want your sausage?"

His ears went up and then one dropped down to the side in a questioning gesture as he started to suckle on the shaft.

Gently Leo pushed him away, but he resisted until the jackal grew firmer in his effort. Finally, Alex sat back on the floor, tail wagging. "What? I've got to earn my meal, don't I?" he growled lustily.

The jackal smirked. "Oh, you'll earn it all right."

Alex's tongue rolled out his muzzle and curled up at the end. "We didn't order stuffed crust, did we?"

The jackal huffed and pulled off his shorts and underwear, discarding them on the ground. "Lie back and you'll find out."

He considered for a moment, not that he didn't want to do it, but to see how worked up he could get Leo. "I mean you did get sausage and pepperoni together," he murmured, lying back with a grin on the area rug in front of the TV. He slipped off his boxers, having to tug his shaft out of them, and tossed the underwear on the couch. He should probably get a towel, but he was too caught up in the moment to care. If they got spots on the rug, they'd worry about that later.

Leo fished out the bottle of lube stashed in the end table drawer, then got down on all fours, creeping over to Alex. He tugged up the fox's shirt. "Hands over your head."

Obediently, Alex compiled. He started to pull off the shirt, but Leo stopped him, leaving it wrapped around his wrists as makeshift handcuffs by pinning the fabric against the ground. If he wanted, Alex could have slipped his hands free, but that wasn't the point. It would give him something to struggle against, and he liked that. The jackal had already found out what made his fur flush.

Hot breath washed over his neck, and a tender play bite nipped at his throat, the jackal's fangs grazing through his fur. Alex gasped in excitement and squirmed as he felt Leo pressing himself up against his rear entrance.

"So, you want sausage?" whispered Leo, muffled, muzzle around Alex's throat. The fox felt a fang graze against his flesh as the jackal waited for his response.

"Yes please," he panted, eyes half closed.

The jackal let go of his neck and had to sit up to open the bottle of lube. He poured a good amount on himself and lubed the fox up by drizzling some over the fox's rump. He then fingered the fox, lubing him up, before climbing back on top, pressing back the fox's already lifted legs so he could fuck him. Alex was already excited and ready, so Leo slipped the tip into the fox's rump easily and gripped his hips as he started to find some leverage.

Once he got himself under Alex, Leo pushed himself in deeper, getting it all the way down into the fox before he started playing with Alex's own member, using his lube slickened paw to stroke the vulpine. Alex moaned as the jackal worked himself in and out.

"Is this what you wanted, foxy?" he said, grabbing Alex's hips and thrusting in, the paw slick with lube matting his fur.

Eyes closed, he panted. "Yes… sir." Leo's knot had started to swell. He'd teased the poor jackal a little too much and he was already worked up.

The jackal slammed himself down into the fox. "Louder."

"Yes, sir." He moaned.

"I want the neighbors to hear you," huffed Leo, his swelling knot making the resistance grow as he slammed in again.

Alex screwed his eyes shut, tugging against the t-shirt wrapped around his hands. "Yes, sir!"

That was all it took, and the jackal forced himself in, the knot tying them together. The fox's cock was already rock hard, and as the jackal's paw closed around the vulpine shaft again, Leo began stroking, grinding his tied member into the fox. This made Alex quiver and tense, causing Leo to finally cum inside the fox.

"Oh god…" the fox panted.

"Come on, I want to feel you twitch around my shaft and milk it," panted Leo.

The fox moaned loudly and shivered at the touch as his knot was squeezed. The jackal stroked quickly, leaning over the fox as he did, and in no time, Alex had shot, getting cum on Leo's shirt.

"That's a good boy," said Leo, leaning back a little and smiling. He smacked Alex's rump causing the fox to jump and yelp and tug against the knot.

"Hey! No abusing the goods."

"You are saying you don't like it a little rough?"

"Mm…" He wiggled his hips, feeling the knot still inside of him. "You aren't supposed to know that."

The jackal leaned forward, still tied to the fox and shifted his weight, so he could bring his muzzle close to the fox and whisper into one of his ears. "Oh, but I do."

The fox smirked. "Well, maybe I want you to know. It makes it more fun."

"You get me in trouble with that, you know."

"Oh please, like the neighbors don't know," he said, tail wagging under them. "It's still early anyway."

Leo shrugged. He was going to say something else, but the doorbell suddenly rang. "Oh shit, they're already here!" hissed the jackal.

"I thought you said they were going to be take thirty minutes," yelped Alex as Leo tugged himself free of the fox, his knot still swollen. It came loose with a squelching sound.

"They're only a few blocks away," said the jackal, grabbing his shorts and dragging them up over his shaft and sheath. The doorbell rang again, and he glanced at his shirt with dried cum still on it. "Shit."

"Use my shirt," said the fox freeing it from his hands and tossing it up to the jackal.

Quickly Leo pulled off the sticky shirt, throwing it aside, and pulled on the other t-shirt. It was a little tight on him, but the pizza guy wouldn't care. He snatched the wallet off the coffee table and walked over to the door. Alex strategically stayed where he was since that part of the living room wasn't visible from the entranceway.

When the jackal opened it, a raccoon was there, holding a pizza box. She took in his disheveled appearance and wrinkled her nose, catching the scent of sex in the air. "One large works for Leonard?"

"Yeah, that's me," said Leo, pulling out money for a tip. "Here you go."

She took the five dollars and passed over the pizza, backing away. The scent coming out of the apartment was strong. "Have a good night."

"You too." Leo closed and locked the apartment door, then came back over to the couch, putting the pizza on the coffee table. "Maybe we should clean up first before we eat."

"Yeah," said the fox, getting up from the floor. Glancing down, he saw there was a lube stain on the carpet. He didn't want to drip on anything, so he curled his tail tight around himself so he could walk to the bathroom.

"Hey Alex?" said the jackal, as the fox was turning away. "Yeah?"

"I grabbed your wallet by accident to tip the driver."

"Oh, that's okay."

He held out the wallet and pulled out two twenty-dollar bills. "I thought you said you were broke."

"Oh, huh, look at that," said the fox with a grin. "I guess I'm not broke."

"Did you… just set me up?"

The grin widened. "Leo, why would I do that?"

The jackal blinked. "You little shit! You just took a dick for delivery."

The fox shrugged. "So I bottomed for pizza. I mean yeah, I could have just ordered pizza myself, but this was a lot more fun, wouldn't you say? Anyway…" he licked his lips. "I wanted sausage tonight."

"You pizza slut."

Alex laughed as he walked toward the bathroom. "Wait till you see what I'll do when you order all the meats. You're going to love that."

After the last story, I couldn't leave well enough alone. Making it Fit is the sequel to Foxing for Pizza and gives us a more in-depth look at the characters. This too has foxing in it. It debuted on my Patreon in 2021.

Making it Fit

As Alex went to pick up the can of pineapple juice to finally fix himself a drink, it slipped out of his paw and went sliding across the table, spilling its contents.

"Fuck!" exclaimed the red fox, as he tried to grab it. His claws scraped across the can, ripping the paper label. He managed to catch it before it hit the ground, but not before most of the can's contents had leaked across the table's wooden surface. Worse, not a drop of juice had landed in his glass.

Pissed at himself, he tossed the can into the sink next to the mixing bowl and sighed. He could open a new can, but he needed to clean the table before Leo got home with dinner. In a moment of 'fuck it', he leaned down and started lapping at the puddle of juice. He was halfway through getting it all up when a sound caught his attention.

"Ahem."

Alex's ears swiveled forward, and he looked up from the table, tongue still against the wooden surface. His roommate, Leo, was standing there holding a plastic bag with four take-out containers in it. He was just staring at the fox.

"Oh, you're home already," Alex said, trying to play it off as he stood up.

The black-backed jackal blinked and then coughed. "Do I want to know why you're licking the kitchen table while naked."

"No," said the fox, "you do not."

"And why are you hard?" asked the jackal, putting the food on the counter away from the fox.

Was he hard? He glanced down and saw the pink tip sticking out of his sheath. "I got excited I guess," replied Alex.

"You get off licking the table now?"

"No! It wasn't that."

"For garlic knots then? You got hard over the garlic knots?"

"Well, they are called knots…" said the fox, the edge of his muzzle curling up.

"I'm going to need a new roommate," mumbled Leo. He went over to the sink and stopped short. "And what the fuck are you doing to our kitchen?" he said, pointing to the flour dust on the counter.

"Working on something for later in the week and making myself a drink."

"Right?" The jackal picked up the empty can. "Is there a reason you are drinking pineapple juice?"

The fox's ears lowered. "It's supposed to improve the taste."

Leo blinked. "Of the table? It improves the taste of the table?"

"Of other things."

"Other things?" He opened his mouth and then his eyes went wide. "What?"

Alex walked over and grinned at Leo, making sure to get close to the jackal so his erection could brush his hip. "Yes, the taste of that."

"You crazy fucking fox, I am not sucking you off right now."

"True, but you did bring garlic knots…."

"Dude, no," said Leo, pushing him away. "Go masturbate or something. We are not having sex tonight."

"You said that last night."

The jackal sighed. "Look, just because you get to work from home and are bored doesn't mean I'm not tired from dealing with shit at the store."

The fox growled. "You think my job isn't hard? You think dealing with irate customers all day on the phone is fun? At least some of yours are friendly."

Leo huffed. "I'm not trying to imply that."

"Then what are you implying?"

Leo sighed. "Look, I'm sorry. I don't want to upset you. I just had a rough day. Let's eat and I will probably go crash on the couch or something when we're done."

The fox regarded him carefully. "You make it sound like I just use you for sex."

The jackal dug into the takeout bag and pulled out two trays of garlic knots. "Sex and food."

"Now, now. I'm quite capable of ordering my own meals."

He rolled his eyes. "Fine, but can you go put some clothing on? All you're doing is flashing your semi-hard shaft around the kitchen."

"What, is it too distracting for you?"

"I don't want to see you dip your sausage into the knots."

"Dude, it's food!" said the fox.

"That hasn't stopped you from dreaming of sausage before," said Leo, fishing utensils out of the drawer and handing them to Alex.

"So I got a little carried away…"

"…and started licking the table."

Alex's ears drooped. "Look, I spilled some pineapple juice, and I didn't want to let it go to waste."

The jackal shrugged and walked over to the table. "You licking the table isn't the weirdest thing you've done." He ran a padded finger across the surface. "But it's still sticky."

"Let me clean it correctly," said the fox, as the jackal went over to the fridge to get a drink.

"Why is there a giant lump of white stuff in the fridge?"

"Oh! That's my new cooking experiment. I'm trying to make pizza dough so we can cook it in that fancy toaster oven you got," said the fox, pointing to the large kitchen appliance that sat on the far end of the counter. "It toasts, it air fries, it does all sorts of stuff."

The jackal closed the door. "I guess we won't be doing as much delivery anymore."

"It's healthier to cook at home," said Alex, as he wiped the table down. "Why do you look so disappointed? My cooking isn't that bad now."

"It's not your cooking I mind."

"What is it then?"

He shrugged. "It's nice when you call me at the end of the day. It helps me disconnect."

The fox grinned as he sat down, the table now clean. "You like picking up dinner, don't you?"

Leo brought the food over from the counter. "Maybe, but you still owe me for the last two times."

"You didn't pay your half of the groceries I got yesterday."

"Crap," said Leo, sitting down. "We're going to need to write this all down, don't we?"

"We should, but how about a wager for who's got next?"

The jackal had just opened his container of pasta. "A wager?"

"Sure, something fun," Leo popped open the first tray of garlic knots. "We've got a dozen knots, right?"

Alex nodded, so Leo continued. "The challenge is simple. Let's see how many knots we each can handle at once. Whoever takes the most knots, wins. The loser gets next."

"I told you, I'm tired. I am not fucking you."

The fox leaned over the table, tail wagging. "Well, that puts me at a disadvantage then, doesn't it? That's one knot I can't take," he said picking up one of the pieces of bread. The smell of the cheese and butter tickled at his muzzle.

"It still leaves you with a complete advantage because I want to taste my food, not shove it all into my muzzle at once."

"Fine, fine. No adventures with knots for us tonight."

The jackal leaned back in his chair and picked up one of the knots. "How many of these do you think you can handle at once anyway?"

"Five, maybe six? I'm sure if I just shove them in, it wouldn't be hard really."

"Tell you what, I've got one for you. You can eat your knots, and if you can eat six before I distract you, I've got next."

"That doesn't seem challenging at all."

"Try me. Let's see if you take all six knots at your leisure without choking on them," said Leo with a grin.

Alex shrugged and took a bite out of the first. "If you're that determined to pay for—hey!" He yelped in surprise as there was a thump under the table.

Leo grinned. "What's the matter foxy? Not sure you can handle it?" he said, as he dragged his foot paw across Leo's crotch.

"That's cheating!"

The jackal grinned. "You didn't ask the rules of the challenge. Now, finish your knots, otherwise you've got dinner next. And you're still a little worked up so you better hurry. I'm sure you'll be showing more in a minute."

Alex went to take another bite, and then grimaced. "Hey hey! Watch where those claws are going."

"Ohh… I can really make this worse now," said Leo, as he bumped the table with his leg.

Alex growled at the slow scrape of Leo's pad across his sensitive tip. "Okay, okay, you win."

"Damn it, this is fun though," said Leo.

"For you!"

Leo dropped his foot. "Fine, I thought you had more stamina than that."

Alex reached down to adjust himself. "You really need to see what you are doing with those claws."

"I guess that wasn't a fair deal then."

Alex just popped the rest of his half-eaten garlic knot into his muzzle in response and started opening his pasta up.

"Why did we order this many knots anyway?"

The fox shrugged. "They're good? That fancy oven will heat up any leftovers nicely."

The jackal picked one up. "It's not because you want to get knot stuffed?"

Alex squinted. "Maybe, but I got a toy for that when I feel needy and you're busy."

Leo sighed and bit into the buttered bread. "Work sucked today, you know. I had this one guy who couldn't make up his mind on what type of phone he wanted. He sucked up an hour of my time, and I didn't even get a sale from him."

"It happens. I had a woman who screamed at me for twenty minutes straight because she misread her bill."

"Didn't that happen last month?"

"Yeah, I think it's the same woman."

The jackal sighed. "Work, we do it so we can afford to live, and what does it ask in return? It takes up a lot of our waking time and takes away many of the best years of our lives. If we're lucky, we can afford to retire and do the things we want to do, hopefully while we still have the energy to do them."

"Yes, it does, but if we're smart, we can still fit in the things we love. I know some people want to leave the modern world behind and run off to the woods, but there are only so many woods out there to go around."

They sat in silence then, eating their pasta.

"Are we getting old?" asked Leo, after a minute of just munching.

"We're all getting older now."

"Yes, but five years ago when I graduated college, I didn't think this would be where I ended up. It was supposed to be easier to make a living."

"Hey, I'm not that bad a roommate now, uh, pineapple juice aside."

Leo shook his head. "Not you, but the tiredness, the exhaustion, and the frustration. Adulting sucks, and not in a good way. I know we're both doing fine, but neither of us can afford to move out on our own off what we make."

"Living alone is lonely though," Alex replied. "Plus, if I lived alone, I wouldn't have the money to go out after work. I'd basically be regulated to whatever small place I could afford on my own."

"Yeah." Leo looked down at his half-eaten food. "I guess I need to do something exciting in my life."

"There you go," said Alex. "Be assertive about being happy."

The jackal got up and walked over to the fox. He leaned against Alex's chair. "You're right, I can't let life beat me down. Also, you've got marinara sauce in your fur."

"I do?" He looked down at his chest. "Where is… mmph!" Alex said, as Leo wrapped a paw around his muzzle.

"Right here," said the jackal, sticking two digits into Alex's food and then rubbing some sauce on his chest fur. He let go and leaned down. "Let me get that for you."

"We were just having a serious conversation!" protested the fox.

"Yeah, well I can't fix the fucking world, but I can make one person happy, and you told me to be assertive." He licked at the fox's chest fluff. "Tell me you don't like it."

The fox shivered. "I hate you know me this well sometimes." Teeth teased at one of his nipples. "Way too well."

"You're complaining?" asked the jackal, before he dragged his tongue across the fox's upper chest. A paw slid across Alex's stomach, reaching down to wrap fingers around his sheath.

"No," said Alex, as he squirmed in his roommate's grasp. "Just surprised."

The jackal chuckled as he trailed his muzzle up the fox's chest so he could whisper in his ear, cheek to cheek. "You being excited about knots makes me excited."

A paw tugged at Leo's work shirt as a digit undid the top button and moved lower. "Who said I was taking it this time?"

"I can be persuasive."

Small sharp teeth teased the edge of the jackal's ear as more buttons on his work shirt were undone. "So can I."

A paw squeezed at the fox's hardening member. "I believe I have you at a disadvantage."

The fox squirmed. "Yes, but..." He placed a hand on the jackal's chest. "We didn't order sausage pizza tonight, we ordered garlic knots."

"Right..." the jackal said, before he leaned down and licked at the fox's neck, who instantly raised his muzzle to point toward the ceiling. Gently he nipped at his neck.

"Oh, fuck you," said Alex with a gasp.

There was a muffled laugh. "Not tonight, foxy."

The fox whined in the jackal's grasp. Leo licked and then nibbled at his neck gently. Alex's shaft was fully out of his sheath now, and he tickled teasingly at it, feeling the way it made the fox twitch. His own erection strained against his work pants. If he kept this up, the fox would easily cum here in the kitchen, but that's not what Leo wanted.

He broke off from the nibbling and let the fox get some composure. "Come on, I've got a surprise for you in my bedroom."

The fox's ears perked. "For me? Shouldn't it wait?"

The jackal grinned. "It's something we can use right now."

The fox's eyes went wide. "You bought me a sex toy!" he exclaimed. "Wait, you bought me a sex toy?"

The jackal's tail wagged as he turned to head down the hall. "Maybe! You'll find out."

Alex looked at his half-eaten food and hesitated for just a second before following. He could always reheat the pasta later.

Leo's room looked like a cross between a high school kid's bedroom and an office. A desktop computer with a headset sat on one side of the room while a queen bed with posters for the bands Danger Box and Nighthowl hung over it. The jackal first pulled off his work pants and kicked them off before he sat down on his bed. Alex had already undone most of the buttons on his shirt with nimble precision, so he finished the job.

"I've been thinking this would be fun, but I don't know if I should give it to you," he said, fishing out a rectangular cardboard box from his nightstand, which he handed to Alex.

The fox looked at the box. It had no markings on it, but it had a lid that easily popped off. He lifted it and his eyes went wide. "You bought me padded leather handcuffs?"

The jackal's ears lowered a little. "Is that too direct? You get so excited when I hold your hands to your side, plus I've seen your porn."

The fox pulled them out of the box and put the box on the dresser. "The center strap disconnects, I see."

"They sell them with locking plates, but I didn't think that was a step we should be taking…" He looked down at the floor. "Sorry, it was a bad—"

"A locking plate would be too much, but I can work with this. I could pretend I'm not that type of boy, but I am." He disconnected one of the cuffs and undid the leather strap. He paused and tilted his head. "I've seen your porn too. These aren't just for me, are they?"

The jackal looked away. "Not exactly, no…"

"Do you want to try them on?"

Leo's ears went up and then down, and then back up. "I… don't think I'm ready for that."

Alex started to fit the cuff on his wrist. "Next time, you should wear them, but I'm game for tonight."

The jackal grinned and pulled the fox over to him. "So, does pineapple juice really improve the taste?"

"I don't know. We can find out, but with these, I'm thinking you had other intentions than oral tonight."

"I do, but I've got a plan. Think you're up for a ride?"

The fox licked his fangs. "A plan you say?"

The jackal grinned and reached out to run a hand along the fox's hip. "Hey, I'm not all just, 'if it fits, shove it in,' now." The paw traced through Alex's fur to his groin. Furred digits tickled up the fox's length. "Not to say that the prospect of a bit of shoving doesn't entice the both of us."

Alex shivered as he tightened the second cuff on his other wrist. "You tease."

Leo let go and laid back on the bed, letting his stiff member float above his stomach. "I'm not teasing. It's yours if you want it."

"Mmm…" The fox got on the bed and placed his paws on either side of Leo's chest. "And what is this plan you have?" asked the fox, rubbing his shaft against the jackal's. "Is this it?"

A paw wrapped around the fox's shaft and his own, "Close, but not quite. Something more… insertive."

Alex's tail wagged playfully, thrusting into the paw. "This isn't enough for you?"

"It would be, but you are the one wearing handcuffs."

The fox licked his lips and lifted up the paw holding the connecting strap. "That's true," he clicked the strap on one of the rings and put his hands behind his back, straddling his roommate. "Like this?"

The jackal grinned and squeezed both of them before he let go to reach for the lube. "Yes."

Alex clicked the other end of the strap to his wrist and tugged. His hands were now restrained behind his back unless he released himself. "Okay, and oh!" he exclaimed, as the jackal snuck a slickened finger into the fox's rump. "I see."

Leo grinned and pulled his paw away. He scooted down the bed just a little so he could position the fox over himself. "Ready?" he asked, as he rubbed the tip of his shaft against the fox's butt.

"You need more lube first."

The jackal pulled his hand away. He squirted some more lube onto his paw before he returned his digits back under the fox to slick himself up. "Better?"

The fox let the shaft rub up against the cleft of his ass for a few seconds, before he sat up and tried to position himself properly.

"You need help?" asked Leo, as the fox worked himself over the tip.

"I got this," said Alex, as the jackal slipped out of him. With annoyance he used his cuffed hands to position Leo's shaft correctly before he sat down, it finally slipping in. "See," he said with a huff. "I know what I'm doing."

He gave an amused bark and pushed up, making the fox gasp. With the fox now hilted, Leo returned his fingers to the fox's shaft. "We both do." The jackal's tail thumped against the bed.

Alex whined and tried to pull his hands around his body, but all he could do was tug on the cuffs as the jackal continued to thrust into him. With increasing urgency, the Leo started to grind himself into the fox.

"Someone is enjoying themself," Leo panted.

His roommate just moaned loudly in response, riding the jackal.

"Come on, give it to me," said Leo, stroking at the fox's hard cock and its swelling knot as it bounced on his stomach.

"Soon," panted Alex, feeling the tension in himself rising.

The jackal pressed on, feeling his own knot starting to grow. "I like a challenge, you know."

The fox whimpered in pleasure as the other male kept pushing himself in and out, trying to tie with him. Alex was attempting to work the jackal's shaft in rhythmic motions, but he was quickly losing control of the situation. As he strained against the cuffs, Leo took what he wanted at his own pace, and that drove the fox crazy.

Finally, Leo tied with him. Together they came; fox cum splattered the jackal's chest, while inside of him, the jackal released his pent-up seed. Alex came so hard, some of his jizz even got on Leo's muzzle.

Contented, they collapsed back against the bed and panted for a moment. Alex was stuck on top of his roommate, but his shoulders sagged in exhaustion. Finally, after he caught his breath, Leo licked his muzzle clean. "Hmm… it tastes the same."

Tongue rolling out of his mouth, the fox said, "I'm sure it takes some time."

Leo squeezed the hard knot and another bit of cum squirted from the fox's throbbing shaft. Slowly he shifted, grinding the tie inside his friend. "Was this what you wanted when you had garlic knots on your mind?"

His tail wagged, and the fox tried to sit up, testing the tie with the jackal. "Yes."

"I know sometimes I don't always have time, but I'm glad I could fit you into my schedule."

Alex rolled his eyes. "Like what else were you going to do tonight?"

The jackal grinned and with great effort and a yip from the fox, he shifted to the side of the bed. "Hey, my hands are still tied here."

"You can release yourself anytime you want," said Leo, as he reached into the drawer and pulled out a dildo which he held up for Alex to inspect.

"You really are planning how you want to fuck me now," said the fox, looking at the canine toy with its knot.

"This one isn't for you."

"Oh… so THAT'S what you do when I'm not home."

The jackal's ears laid back. "Not always. Plus, I'm tight."

The fox grinned. "I can fix that," he said, finally fidgeting with the cuffs and undoing them. "Give me the toy, and the lube."

"We just…" Leo's eyes screwed shut as Alex shifted his weight, still tied to the jackal. "Okay, okay, don't yank me around like that."

The fox smiled and squirted lube onto the toy. "Just to the knot."

The jackal whined, "Alex, I'm not ready for that yet."

"How much did you take on your own?"

The jackal sighed. "I keep getting stuck with the knot."

"It's different when it grows on you instead of having the entire thing to work with to start," Alex wiggled his hips. "You're not going to have a better distraction to help you relax than this."

The jackal nodded sheepishly.

"Let me know if it's too much," said the fox, and he carefully positioned the toy, holding his tail to the side to keep it out of the way. "You're going to need to lift your legs." Already he could tell the tie with the jackal was weakening, and if he tried, he could pull himself off, but it would hurt. Anyway, he couldn't let the canine out yet if this was going to work.

Obediently, Leo lifted his legs and with a yip from the fox, and a grunt from himself, they got their tied selves in a position where Leo's legs were bent at the knees.

He didn't have a lot of leverage since the position was kind of awkward, but the Alex gently lubed up the jackal's ring of muscles, sticking a digit in before pulling it out.

"Concentrate on me," said the fox, and he started to press the toy against the jackal's ass.

Leo's paw returned to his shaft and he squeezed. Alex wasn't completely hard, but he felt that send a shiver up his spine. Carefully, he slipped the toy in slowly, while the jackal grunted.

"It's too big," whined Leo.

The fox shifted his hips. "Come on, stick with me here. If I can do this, you can too."

"I'm trying."

The fox pressed on, feeling the toy sink into the jackal before pulling it halfway out. "Focus on me," said the fox, giving a little bounce on the jackal's shaft.

Leo gave a needy whine. "Oh, my dog," he said, stroking the fox.

"You can do this," huffed Alex. Leo's stroking was already returning him to attention as he started to press the knot against the jackal with each thrust of the toy. Suddenly he felt the jackal buck underneath him, and he pushed deeper with the dildo.

"Oh wow, I think I'm going to cum again!" exclaimed Leo.

The sudden penetration by the toy was too much for him and the jackal jerked, coming again, still buried in the fox. His stroking slacked off, the fox's aching member still hard but not spent a second time.

"There we go. Your toy fits nicely inside of you," remarked Alex with a smirk, his tail wagging. He'd hilted the toy right inside of Leo as he'd cum.

The jackal whined. "You can take that out now."

"Not until you finish me off," Alex said, thumping his shaft on Leo's chest. "I'm so close to cumming again, you aren't getting away just yet. You need to finish this."

Obediently the jackal started stroking the fox again. The fox panted, enjoying his position on top. Teasingly he twisted the toy slowly, feeling the way it made the jackal twitch.

"Hey, I don't do stuff like that to you."

"Yes," panted the fox, trying to thrust into the jackal's paw, "you do."

The jackal's ears went back. "You like that though."

The fox shook his head and closed his eyes, deciding to just rest his hands on his legs and leave the toy alone. "I still haven't forgotten the ice cube trick you pulled on me."

Leo didn't say anything and just kept tugging at the fox's cock. It only took a little bit longer before Alex came again, this time not as strongly, but enough to add to the mess on the jackal's stomach.

Tiredly, the fox pulled himself off of his friend and plopped himself onto his back on the bed next to him.

"You forget something?"

"Oops!" Alex got back up on his knees and gently pulled the toy out of the jackal. "Uh, we made a mess of your sheets."

"I'll change them. The comforter will need to be washed, but I'll be fine without it tonight."

"So, you still worried I won't need you if I start cooking pizza at home?"

The jackal rolled over and looked at him. "Not really, but I still don't know how to cook."

Alex leaned forward to give Leo a soft kiss. "That's okay. There will be dishes to wash."

"Wonderful…"

"I'm sure we'll still have some takeout in our schedule. I can't cook every night now."

"No?" Leo's muzzle quirked up. "You seem good at fitting things in that are important to you."

The fox traced a finger up the jackal's spent shaft. "Oh, I can always fit you into my schedule now, but can you fit me in is the question."

The jackal gave the fox a sly grin. "Make me some pizza tomorrow, and we'll see if I can."

Splatters *explores identity and drag. Published in 2016 by FurPlanet in* FANG Volume 7, *this is a story about being down and out and touches on how life happens when we don't expect it to. Sometimes things are messy, but that's okay.*

Splatters

The feeling of the bus slowing down on the interstate off-ramp jolted Jewel awake. The leopard blinked, trying to focus his eyes, but outside there was nothing but the inky blackness of night. The bus pulled up to the end of the ramp and stopped.

"Food stop," said the bus driver, as he took a left and went under the interstate bridge.

Food stop where? There's nothing here, thought Jewel. The only light came from the bus' headlights. Then the coach emerged from under the overpass, and Jewel saw the glow of a truck stop.

"You get thirty minutes," yelled the bear. "Anyone not back on the bus will be left behind, and you don't want that. The next bus won't be through till mid-morning."

Jewel sighed; the last thing the leopard wanted was to get off the bus. She, it was she right now, just wanted to get home. Then Jewel could go back to being Jawell and slip off his dress. It would be a weekend he could joke about with friends after he got through it.

The ocelot next to Jewel yawned, having dozed off himself. He was shorter than Jewel with long smudged rosettes in his fur unlike Jewel's neatly organized ones. They'd been on the bus together since noon when it had left Amarillo. "Oh good. I'm hungry. You want to eat together?"

The leopard sighed internally and forced his voice a little higher. "I'm not really hungry." The ocelot was nice, but Jewel got the feeling the only reason he kept talking to her on this trip was that he found her attractive.

"You sure?" The ocelot checked his watch. "It's 7:45, and we won't be in Las Vegas till morning."

Jewel smiled, even while his stomach was growling in protest. "I'm sure." He only had five dollars left to his name. Not only had the gig in Texas fallen though, thus denying him the ability to pay next month's rent, but his luggage had been stolen from his cheap motel room. The whole weekend was a waste, and he just wanted to put it behind him. He shouldn't have bothered to go. There were more opportunities for him to perform in Vegas than in Texas.

The bus jerked to a halt in the back of the truck stop, and the passengers got up as the bus driver opened the door. Chilled air swept into the bus. Some yawned, having dozed off while the bus crossed the deserted desert as night fell. The ocelot got up and turned to Jewel when she didn't move.

"You're not getting off?"

"I'm just tired."

The ocelot flicked his tail. "You should stretch your legs."

Jewel didn't want to go, but that argument was logical. The bus was scheduled to arrive in Las Vegas at 6:30 in the morning. With luck, Jewel's roommate would still be up after bartending all night and willing to get her so she could go back to being a he. Hopefully the laughing wouldn't start until they got out of the bus station. After that, Jawell could work on figuring out how he was going to pay next month's rent in a few days with his promised performance fee now out of the question.

"Yeah," she said, getting up. "I should."

The ocelot held out a hand, and reluctantly Jewel took it as he helped her out of the window seat. Jewel grabbed the backpack carrying what little she still had with her, unwilling to let it go. They were the last two to get off the bus before the bus driver did.

"Thirty minutes," reminded the bear.

"No problem," replied the ocelot, and Jewel nodded. The two felines walked toward the building with its fluorescent and neon lighting. The smell of food coming from the attached burger joint made Jewel's stomach grumble.

"You sure you don't want something to eat?" asked the ocelot, picking up on the sound.

Jewel looked at him. He looked genuinely concerned. "I don't have the money. I used the last of my money to pay for my bus ticket."

"Oh! I'm happy to pay for a pretty girl like you," he smirked.

Jewel caught the wink in his eye. "Thank you," she said, as she followed him inside into the fast-food restaurant. Many of the bus's passengers were already in line. The subtle brush of the ocelot's hand against Jewel while they waited in line only concerned him further. The tickle of male arousal in his nose felt like a warning. The leopard wondered if this is what his female friends had to always deal with when they told guys no. At least this would be a short stop. Back on the bus, she could catch some sleep.

�

His mother had told him she didn't mind if he was gay. He was one of six and his sisters had big families. Him doing drag—that was something she'd been a bit more suspicious about. "Just because you like to be with a man doesn't mean you have to look like a woman, Jawell," had been her catch phrase. "Its easy money, and I love the feeling of liberation," always was his response. Right now, it didn't feel liberating at all.

"For a girl, you sure can eat," the ocelot commented with a laugh.

Jewel ears reddened a little. Maybe it was blowing his cover, but she'd ordered a double cheeseburger and a large fry. It was the first substantial meal he had eaten since Saturday morning, and he resolved to at least enjoy it.

"I'm just famished," said the leopard. Jewel had her legs crossed. The male part of him was pretty sure the bulge in the front of the dress was obvious if you looked, so he consciously tried to keep it hidden. He considered tucking before he'd gotten on the bus, but he knew sitting for hours tucked would have been uncomfortable. The dress itself, a single-piece pullover, at least hid some of his bulky frame. If he ever did find out who had stolen his suitcase, he wanted to go all the way back to Texas to knock them around a bit.

"So, what are you doing heading to Las Vegas?" asked the ocelot.

"I'm going home."

"Oh, cool. I'm heading to Las Vegas for a job. Things weren't working for me back in Oklahoma City, and Las Vegas has a lot more opportunities. I wanted to fly, but it's so much cheaper to take the bus, and I had the time."

Jewel thought back to his last steady gig. It had been as a waiter in a restaurant that only employed drag queens. The work had been tiring and thankless. The tips hadn't been good either. "Las Vegas isn't always milk and honey."

"Yeah, but it's easier to find something than in Oklahoma. They're always doing something new in Vegas."

She nodded and crammed some more fries into her muzzle.

"We never introduced ourselves formally on the bus. My name is Christian. What's your name?"

"Oh," she mumbled, "It's Jewel."

"That's pretty."

Jewel just crammed more fries into her muzzle. This would be easier if she let him do most of the talking, and he didn't disappoint.

❧

The bus driver didn't look happy. He was standing by the bus with everyone gathered around. For the last ten minutes he'd been cursing up a storm over the radio while the passengers stood outside.

"Dispatch says they can get a new bus here in the morning, but for the moment we're stranded here. I told them they needed to check this damn thing out."

"What's wrong with it?" asked a weasel near the front of the crowd.

"Not sure. I've tried to get it to start, but the engine isn't turning over. I told them back in Texas the last driver said she was running rough."

"So, we're just stuck here?" someone asked.

The bus driver grunted. "Yeah. Right here in the middle of nowhere."

"And what does dispatch expect us to do?" inquired the weasel.

"Nothing. The fast-food place inside is twenty-four hour, and there is a hotel across the highway," the bear remarked, pointing to a ramshackle looking motel. The vacancy sign was on, but some of the letters were burned out. It just read "Va—ncy" now.

"They're paying for rooms, aren't they?" someone asked.

The bear shook his head. "Nope."

People stirred, the reality setting in. "It's a mechanical problem! They should have checked the bus!" "What do you mean we don't get rooms? I want a refund!"

The bear cleared his throat. "Look, it's company policy, I'm sorry. If we get stuck, we get stuck. People sleep in our stations all the time, and this, in corporate's mind, counts as a station. The relief bus should be here in the morning. Just be back here by 9:30. That's when they're saying we'll do load up. Anyone who wants to get a room at the motel—come with me. I'll get your room numbers down so I know where to find you."

There was an angry grumble in the crowd, but the bus driver held up his hands. "Call corporate and complain. I'll even give you the number. Now, who wants their luggage?"

As a line formed, Jewel stamped her feet. Great, now she couldn't even get home on time. The last time she'd bathed was yesterday and she didn't have any spare clothes. The feminine perfume she'd put on was starting to fade, and her natural male musk would be obvious to anyone standing next to her soon.

"Do you think we could split a hotel room?" Christian asked, as the driver opened one of the luggage compartments.

She didn't want to answer that question, but the answer was easy. "I can't afford that."

"Oh right." Christian frowned. "I'm not sure I can afford a room on my own. I need to make sure I have enough for the hotel room in Las Vegas. If it's not too pricey, I can swing it."

She nodded. "I don't have anything under the bus, so I'm going to go back inside." Jewel wandered off to leave the ocelot to collect his luggage. There was no way under any circumstance she was going to let him get her in a hotel room. Her cover would be blown.

The ocelot glanced after her and got in line to get his bags.

One benefit of the stop was that Jewel finally could charge her cell phone. The broken power outlet for her seat had been another frustration for this already miserable trip. After texting her roommate to let him know about the delay, she let her phone sit undisturbed. The battery was only at fifteen percent, so she wanted to get some juice into it.

At least she still had the book she had been reading, an erotic gay romance she got at the local bookstore back in Nevada. The stud of a horse wrapping his arms around a wolf on the cover made the content a dead giveaway, but it occurred to Jewel that if she was trying to play a convincing woman, reading gay romance wasn't too off the wall. Some straight woman loved a good gay story; there were twice the number of men in it.

He was just getting to a good part, where the wolf took the horse back to his mansion, when Jewel heard a cough that caused her to look up suddenly.

Christian was standing there, towing a rolling suitcase behind himself. "Mind if I join you?"

Jewel put the book down. Glancing at it, she realized she had placed it with the front cover showing. The moment she did that she had to resist the urge to flip the book onto its back.

"Sure. I thought you went to get a hotel room."

"Yeah. They want seventy dollars. I could do thirty-five, but not seventy."

Great, now she was stuck with him. She glanced at the book then back to the ocelot. "That is a bit steep for an old looking motel." When Christian nodded, she rested one of her paws on top of the book to keep him from noticing the cover.

He glanced toward the book then. "Sorry, I guess I'm bothering you. Did you want to read?"

"That's all I have to do."

Christian's ears went back. "Yeah, I understand that. I'm going to go get some bum wine and sit outside and watch the trucks come in. That at least is in my price range, and hopefully nobody cares. It seems most of the people from the bus sprung for hotel rooms. I'll see you in the morning back on the bus."

The leopard nodded. "Yeah." She picked the book back up. "Sounds good."

৵

A fast-food cashier poked at her. "You can't sleep in here," he said to her.

"What?" Jewel mumbled, lifting her head off of the plastic tabletop. "What time is it?"

"You can't sleep in here," said the lanky swift fox. He had to be barely out of high school.

"Sorry, I just dozed off," she yawned, and picked the book back up.

"It's okay, but I'm going to have to ask you to leave," said the fox, crossing his arms.

Great, this is just what she needed. "I don't have anywhere to go. The bus driver locked the bus up. I can't afford the motel across the street."

"Sorry, ma'am. It's company policy. No sleeping in the store."

"Yeah, but this truck stop also doubles as a bus station, doesn't it? The bus company isn't paying for rooms for us."

The fox flicked his ears. "I just know what my boss told me. Sorry."

Jewel picked up her phone. It read 10:47 and was at least fully charged. She unplugged it from the outlet and grabbed her backpack. The fox waited, and when she was ready, he escorted her out of the fast-food seating area to where the soda cases and snacks were. He then turned around and went back to cleaning the seating area.

40

What a load of shit, she thought. Jewel walked outside to get some air. The harsh fluorescent lighting made the entire place feel sterile. All she wanted was to get home. What was so hard about this?

The concrete and pavement were like an island of the modern world in a dark void. The motel with its ramshackle sign stood across the road, but there weren't any other major landmarks nearby. Jewel wasn't even sure exactly what state she was in. She was pretty sure if she waited for a bit, she could go back to the fast-food restaurant. Maybe a cup of coffee would keep her up and at least get her through the night once the fox finished his shift.

On the side of the truck stop overlooking the interstate, she encountered two people. She paused, concerned, but a quick scan told her they weren't a threat. One of them, a weasel from the bus, was sleeping against a trashcan, his bag clutched tightly in his arms. The other just stared off into space, a rolling suitcase propped up against the wall of the building. He sat on the curb, a paper bag clutched in his paws. Jewel's nose quickly told her it was Christian.

"Hey," she said, coming up to the ocelot. Her voice sounded too masculine though, so Jewel made sure to make it higher, back to the tone he normally used in drag. "They just kicked me out of the restaurant," she followed up, hoping to cover up the greeting.

"Oh hey, Jewel," said Christian. "Why did they do that?"

"I fell asleep reading. One of the workers escorted me out."

"Yeah. I've gotten the impression they don't like the bus company stranding us here. I talked about that to our compatriot over there before he decided to catch some shuteye. Want a nip?" said Christian, holding up the paper bag.

Jewel glanced back at the weasel and sat down on the curb, dropping her bag gently on the ground. She made sure to not dirty her dress as she sat down and then took the offered bag.

"Are you keeping an eye out for him?"

"He told me to come wake him when the sun comes up. I figured since I didn't have anything else to do, I might as well."

Jewel nodded and put the bottle up to her nose. The smell of the alcohol was strong, covered by a chemical flavoring. A quick nip confirmed that the contents didn't taste better then they smelled. It burned in the back of Jewel's throat.

"This is… awful."

"Yeah, it is. It's the cheapest thing they had. It's got some kick to it, but I think it tastes like glass cleaner."

"You drink enough of this, you'll go blind."

The ocelot laughed. "It's my second bottle. I should have stopped at one, but I hoped after I felt toasty it would taste better. It doesn't."

Jewel took another nip and wrinkled her nose at the taste. She handed the bottle back to Christian. "I think I'll pass," she coughed.

The ocelot shrugged, and held it up to sniff at the bottle again. "Yeah. It still smells bad." He put the concealed bottle down. "You know, you are the most roll with the punches girl I've ever met."

"What do you mean?" asked the leopard.

"I can tell you know how to make do. It's not something I've seen in many women. I don't know many who would come out here and share a drink with a man down on his luck like me."

Jewel chuckled uneasily. "Perhaps you don't know enough women. I know some lesbians who can take a coat hanger and a pair of pliers and fix a pickup truck. They're not very pretentious."

"My ex was pretty uptight about things. It's part of why I am taking the job in Las Vegas. I wanted to get a fresh start."

"Nevada is pretty different than Oklahoma," Jewel remarked.

The ocelot laughed. "Yeah. I hear it is way more open since they have The Strip and the casinos."

They lapsed into silence as a big rig rolled in from the interchange. The lights of cars and trucks going by on the interstate filled the horizon.

Christian pointed at the highway. "You know, I always wonder where people are going this time of night on a Sunday. Especially this far from anywhere. Are they going home to see loved ones, or just trying to put some miles behind them."

"Who knows?"

Christian chuckled and picked up the bottle. "Man, I want to get out of this place." He was going to take another sip, but he wrinkled his nose when it got close. "Do you want any more of this?"

Jewel shook her head. "Absolutely not. It tastes awful."

The ocelot got up and dumped the contents of the bottle down the drain. "It's a waste of water," he remarked. After he emptied the bottle, he tossed it in a trash receptacle the weasel wasn't sleeping against before returning to sit next to Jewel.

"I'm glad to be able to share this moment with you," he remarked, "no matter how screwed up it is."

Jewel shrugged, and sat quietly watching the distant interstate, both hands resting behind her on the sidewalk. After a minute, she felt a paw resting on one of hers.

"I didn't come out here looking for a hook up," she said bluntly. Christian's scent had changed a little and become sharper. She could tell what his mind had drifted to.

"You're also not like most women I meet, but I understand." He pulled his hand back and looked away, biting his lip. "I don't want to ruin a good moment."

Even though she suspected she knew the answer, Jewel had to ask. "Like most women?"

The ocelot hesitated. "You're not as feminine as most girls I've met. I kind of like that about you. It's refreshing."

This is what I get for talking too much, thought Jewel. "I'm not sure how I should take that."

The ocelot grinned, and in the light of the truck stop, his smile was strangely refreshing. "However you want I guess. To change the topic, what book were you reading? I didn't get a look at it."

"Oh." Jewel blushed. "You wouldn't be interested in it."

"What else is there for us to talk about?"

The leopard's ears twitched nervously. "Well," she sucked in her breath, but no reasonable excuse came to her, so she went with the truth. "It's a gay romance."

The ocelot blinked. "Really?"

The leopard nodded, while the ocelot looked at her perplexed.

"You really aren't like most girls," said Christian, finally.

On this one fact, you are really dense, thought Jewel.

"Yeah, well I'm into that."

"Into?" Christian blinked. "You like to watch? Wait. You're… you're a guy?"

Jewel, or Jawell, nodded. "Yeah," he said using his usual vocal tone.

The ocelot sat stock still. "I just tried to hit on a guy, in a dress, but you don't smell like a guy," he said confused.

"I put female pheromones and perfume on before I went to the bus station," Jawell said.

"Why the hell are you traveling all the way to Nevada in a dress?"

Jawell cleared his throat. "It's not my first choice. I do drag, but my luggage got stolen. This is literally all the clothing I have left."

Christian had a comic expression on his face. "And I just tried to make the move on you. I wanted to ask if maybe you wanted to rent one of the showers." He blushed. Even in the glaring outdoor lighting, the leopard could see the red in his ears.

Jawell got up and dusted off the dress. "I'm not sure many women would take you up on that offer."

He laughed nervously. "I'm pretty sure most would turn me down."

"Then why ask?"

He shrugged. "Boredom, I guess. As I said, you seemed pretty chill, and even now, you're still pretty chill. That's attractive in general."

The leopard twitched his whiskers. "Oh really?"

He bobbed his head. "Yeah. Can I ask you a question?"

"Sure."

He gave a nervous chuckle. "Is it true that men give better head than woman?"

The leopard blinked. "Uh, not sure, but men know the equipment better." Jawell watched how Christian responded to his reply. He didn't seem phased by it. "Why, you still want to try the shower thing?"

Christian sucked in his breath. "I've been curious. I'm willing to give it a go. You are still the same person."

Jawell's tail flicked. "Really?"

The ocelot nodded slowly. "Sure. I mean is it that different? I jerked off with a friend once."

The leopard licked his lips. "So, you think you're man enough to have sex with another man?"

"Man enough?" Christian asked confused.

"Come on," said the leopard, reaching out for the ocelot's paw. Christian took it, and Jawell pulled him up. "Grab your bag," he added, and when Christian did, the leopard led him back into the truck stop. They walked up to the front counter, where a coyote was milling around behind it.

"Hi," said Jawell, using his feminine voice. "My boyfriend and I wanted to rent one of your showers."

The coyote looked them over. "You two were on the bus?" she asked them.

"Yeah," said the leopard. "It's been a long day, and we'd like to clean up. We still have an eleven hour ride in the morning."

The coyote looked at the two and narrowed her eyes. "Right." She walked over to one of the registers. "Shower rental is fourteen dollars. Are either of you drivers?"

They shook their heads. Jawell wondered if Christian was going to try and pull away, but he didn't.

"The showers are standard. You rent them for an hour. You get two towels, bathmat, wash cloth, and of course shampoo." She punched something into her sales terminal. "How did you want to pay?"

Christian broke away and pulled out his wallet. He glanced at Jawell who also pulled his out of his backpack. One thing he admitted that did ruin the traveling girl look is he didn't have a small clutch. He pulled out the five dollars he had and handed them to Christian. The leopard took the five and put down a twenty on the counter.

The coyote took the money and returned the change. She then punched a code into a box next to the cash register. "Your number is thirty-seven," said the coyote. We'll call you in a minute over the intercom," she added, slipping them a key card.

They walked over to the side of the store and browsed some knickknacks while they waited. Christian's tail twitched back and forth nervously, and Jawell waited for him to get cold feet.

"I won't make you go through with this," whispered Jawell to the ocelot.

Christian took a deep breath. "I want this. You're special... Jewel?"

"Jawell actually," said the leopard. "Jewel Starshine is my performing name."

"It's pretty," said Christian. He reached up to touch Jawell's chin. "Jewel seems to suit you. There is a brilliance about you, and even though I can tell you are wise to the world, a little innocence is buried deep down below that shines through."

The leopard blinked. "That innocent look may be why I've never made it as a drag performer. What we are about to do though is anything but innocent."

Christian leaned in and kissed him. Instantly Jawell tensed. The ocelot's breath still smelled of that horrible bum wine, but it made Jawell's privates tingle for more. The panties he had on were starting to lose their limited ability to hide his bulge. When they broke off, they looked at each other, faces still close.

"You've done this before, haven't you?" whispered the leopard.

"Number thirty-seven, your shower is ready," came the voice of the coyote over the intercom. "Shower room three."

Christian took Jawell's hand, and they walked toward the back of the building where a sign saying "Showers" hung over a hallway. "I know how to kiss a pretty lady. That mutual masturbation thing, it did involve some awkward muzzle action."

Jawell perked his ears and wrapped himself around one of Christian's arms before he asked, "And did he go down on you?"

They stopped in front of the door to shower number three, both still toting their luggage. "We both tried it. He didn't like it."

"And you?"

"I am willing to explore the idea further."

Jawell pulled out the key card he'd tucked into his backpack. "This is definitely further, wouldn't you say?"

Christian nodded. "Yeah."

The leopard slid the key card into the lock and it clicked. He opened the door and walked in, the ocelot following behind.

The room was like a bathroom found in a house. Tiled in large neutral colored tile, it had a sink with a vanity, toilet, and a shower in the back. Two towels sat on the vanity. A floor mat hung next to the shower. By the door, there was a bench to put a suitcase on. The room was impeccably clean and had a faint antiseptic smell to it.

"I figured this would be some grimy porn experience," said Christian, as the door swung closed behind them.

"This is actually nice," laughed Jawell, as he looked around. "Wow."

"And for the next hour, it's ours."

Jawell kicked off the shoes he'd been wearing for two days. Free of the sandals, he let his paws rest on the cool tile. Next the leopard reached in and pulled out the false breasts in his bra under the dress.

"Now that is weird," said Christian, as Jawell carefully put them down next to the ocelot's suitcase.

"Hey, it beats using socks. I also didn't ask to have my luggage stolen." He paused. "So, uh, how do you want to do this?"

The ocelot pulled the t-shirt he'd been wearing off and dropped it on the floor. Then he walked over to Jawell and smirked, showing his fangs. The look itself made Jawell itch for the ocelot's touch. "Let's see, oh this has a zipper." He tugged down the zipper in the back as he licked his lips. "Now," he said as he pulled the dress off of Jawell's shoulders, "let's see if this drops."

Jawell squirmed and managed to get the dress over his hips. It fell to the floor. He let the panties he wore drop also, his bulging sheath already showing a pink tip. He lifted the bra over his head and grinned, twirling it around, now naked.

Christian sucked in his breath. "You really are a guy."

"Oh my god, you didn't believe me?"

The ocelot ran a paw along Jawell's side and hip. "Oh, I did."

The leopard shivered at the touch, lashing his tail. "It's good to let it hang out again." He licked his lips and stepped closer to the ocelot, tracing a paw over Christian's hip before reaching down and playing with his sack through the fabric of his pants. "I can blow you right here, if you want."

The ocelot smiled a little nervously. "I would love that," rumbled the feline.

Jawell licked his fangs, backed Christian up against a wall, and got down on his knees. The tile was cool, and he felt like a slut on the floor, which just turned him on more. It had been a while since he'd gotten to blow someone, and he wasn't going to turn that down now. He unbuttoned Christian's pants and pulled them off with the cat's underwear. The ocelot kicked them out of the way.

Christian purred as Jawell pulled down the sheath to reveal the pink shaft underneath. The touch of his rough tongue on it sent shivers up the ocelot, causing his tail to lash. He teased at the tip, before he worked down the shaft a little ways.

"Ooo, you do know your way around down there. My girl never liked giving head."

Jawell reached up to grab a hold of the shaft, before he pulled back. "They'd take my gay card…" He licked at the tip playfully. "If I didn't know how to give a good blow job."

The ocelot panted, and Jawell went back down on him. Christian buried his shaft into the leopard's muzzle with abandon. Jawell lost himself in the sensation. It was instinctual. The throb of Christian's member in his muzzle turned him on and lit fireworks in his mind. Now that he had this, he wanted it badly. Obviously he was too enthusiastic, because Christian pulled out suddenly.

"Ugh, man, ugh, ooh!" He shot his load, splattering Jawell in the face, getting his whiskers and the top of his short muzzle. "Oh man, I didn't mean to get it all over your face," mumbled the ocelot, after he stopped panting so hard.

"No biggie," Jawell said, licking the corner of his muzzle so he could taste Christian's seed. "It's a hazard I'm used to. It comes with the territory."

The ocelot's tail lashed. He blushed as he spoke. "You look so hot in that position. Can I suck you off?"

The leopard blinked and pushed himself off of the floor. "Sure."

"Maybe you can fuck me too; I've played with a dildo before."

Christian was not nearly as straight as Jawell had first thought.

"I can try. You have to be loose. For a first time, that may be too much."

Christian blushed and got down on his knees. "I want to be a pretty kitty like you."

Jawell flashed his fangs and let his half hard erection bob between them. "What would make you a pretty kitty?" he asked.

Christian looked down at the floor. "You getting it all over me."

The leopard smirked and splayed a paw around his cock base. "Open up then."

Hesitantly, the ocelot leaned forward, licking at the shaft. He was clumsy, but after the initial taste on his tongue, he started to get excited. He explored Jawell's shaft, first with his muzzle, and then he pulled back to nuzzle it while he jerked Jawell off.

"I want you to cum," panted Christian, stroking the leopard's penis.

Jawell growled and stepped forward, and Christian went back down on his shaft. "Keep sucking."

"Mmph!" said the ocelot around a mouthful of cock. He sucked down hard and bobbed along the shaft, before he gagged and had to fall back, sprawling across the tile.

Jawell, so close now, panted and stepped over him, jerking himself off. "Who's a pretty kitty?"

"Me!" panted the ocelot, and he opened his muzzle as Jawell came. Cum sprayed down on top of him, some of it falling onto his chest, and some onto his face. A few drops even fell into the cat's eager muzzle. As Jawell panted after his release, he realized Christian was furiously masturbating.

"You want more?" he mumbled.

The ocelot nodded, sprawled across the tile and splattered in cum.

"We'd need lube."

"There is some in my suitcase," said Christian, "in the main compartment."

Jawell walked over and unzipped the suitcase. Inside he found clothes and a few papers.

"It's tucked into the top."

Jawell reached in and felt his paw brush across something smooth and silicone. He clasped his paw around it and pulled out a small canine toy. Underneath it he found a small bottle of lube. Getting up, he smirked and walked back over to the ocelot.

"This is yours?" he said teasingly, holding the dildo up.

The ocelot nodded.

Jawell popped open the bottle of lube and poured some onto the toy. He proceeded to slick it up. "Does someone still want to try anal?"

Christian had his eyes fixed needfully on the toy. He sucked in his breath. "Yes."

The leopard lashed his tail and licked the side of his muzzle. He knelt down next to the ocelot who lifted his legs up. He smeared lube against the ocelot's pucker. Immediately the ocelot pulled his legs back further and yowled. Not sparing Christian, he slipped a digit into the other feline as his free hand drizzled lube onto Christian's shaft. He then pulled out a finger and lined up the canine toy as he used his other hand to grip Christian's rock-hard cock.

When the ocelot quivered, he pushed the toy in, expecting to meet resistance. Instead, it sank in easily to the knot. Jawell started to pump it in and out of him.

"Oh my god, oh my god!" purred the ocelot in ecstasy.

"You like that?" asked Jawell.

He nodded and then whined, "I'm so going to come." A hand reached out to grip Jawell's shaft which was only half hard. "I don't want to cum before you fuck me."

The leopard paused. He didn't plan to actually fuck the ocelot. The lube and toy should be enough to get him over the edge and fully spent.

"Please?" whined Christian.

"Are you sure?" asked the leopard.

In response the ocelot pushed himself across the tile with his free arm so his rough tongue could dart across the tip of Jawell's half hard erection.

"Mmph," whimpered Jawell as the tongue touched his sensitive flesh. Christian got the tip against his nose and kissed it. As Christian suckled on the tip, the leopard could feel himself getting fully hard again. "Fine," he purred. "I'll do it."

Christian let go and Jawell pulled the toy out of him. He had to crawl over the other cat and slick himself up with the lube. He then proceeded to slip into the already loosened ocelot, who bucked his hips up when he was entered.

Wrapping both arms against Christian's legs, Jawell proceeded to pound him. The ocelot's tail lashed, and his breathing became ragged. The small barbs at the base of the leopard's penis caused Christian to cry out.

He pushed himself into the ocelot, building up a hurried rhythm. He hadn't been this aroused in ages, and he kept pushing forward with building urgency. Christian just panted raggedly, body twitching in pleasure. When Jawell started to masturbate him, the ocelot exploded in his gripping paw. The leopard pulled out as the other feline collapsed against the tile, purring.

Even though he'd just climaxed, it didn't take Jawell long before he came a second time, painting Christian's furry sack and his finally softening shaft with leopard cum.

Collapsing back, he huffed, trying to catch his breath. The ocelot was covered in spooge, spent and panting against the tile floor.

"Are you still a pretty kitty?" whispered Jawell. It seemed liked a silly question, but he wanted to hear the answer.

Christian leaned his head off the floor so he could look at Jawell and smirked. "Oh god yes," he breathlessly said before he lowered his head against the tile. "I'm so glad we get to take a shower now."

৵

They showered together, during which Christian had been intimate, but a little aloof. He'd responded to Jawell's touch slowly, almost methodically. Jawell expected that, and he could tell the other feline was having to process what just happened. The bathmat had come in handy since they'd made a real mess on the floor. After the shower, Jawell brushed his fur while he watched Christian preen in the mirror.

"So," he asked. "How do you feel now?"

The ocelot paused and looked back at him. "That was intense."

"It had been awhile for me." Jawell picked up his dress and sighed. He really didn't want to put this back on and be Jewel right now.

"Same here. I'm going to need to think this through," said the ocelot. "I mean that was fun, but I don't know."

Jawell felt his ears droop a little and his tail sagged. He wasn't sure how Christian would feel about what they'd done after it sunk in. "Are you going to be okay?" he asked hesitantly.

The ocelot finished zipping up a clean pair of pants and paused to look at Jawell.

"It's… it's different. I've never done something this involved with a guy. I mean, I jerked one off, and I have used the toy on myself, but this… this is very different."

"Did you find it hot?" asked the leopard.

The ocelot turned around to pick up a shirt, so Jawell couldn't see his face. The leopard wrung his paws.

"Did you find it hot?" he asked again.

Christian turned to look at him. "That was the most intense sexual experience of my life. I always thought of myself as a man's man. I knew when I got the toy and tried it, I had a gay streak in me, but I never thought it ran that deep."

"Just because you like men doesn't mean you're any less of a man."

The ocelot slipped the shirt over himself. "That wasn't a man's way of having sex. That—"

"It's called being a bottom. I'm not saying you can't top, but you obviously enjoy being a bottom."

The other cat blushed red. "I need to think," said Christian, and turned to close up his suitcase. Jawell still hadn't put the dress on and was standing naked in front of him.

"Christian, look, I'm sorry. It's no big deal. One gay experience isn't the end of your life. Some guys are bisexual."

The ocelot looked back. "I'm going for a walk, down the road."

The leopard felt himself shrink back. "Sure," he said finally.

"Thanks," the ocelot whispered as he left the shower, wheeling his suitcase behind him. Jawell stared at the door for a few minutes before he put the dress on.

ॐ

The relief bus sat next to the original bus in the early morning light. Jewel stood there holding her backpack as everyone got on board. She didn't see Christian in the line for the bus.

"Twenty-one, twenty-two, twenty-three," the bus driver said pointing to Jewel who was last in line. He checked his notes on a battered clip board as Jewel dawdled by the door to the bus. The bus driver waved Jewel on. She got on the bus and took a seat in an empty row. The bus driver got on and recounted how many people he had.

"I had twenty-four when we pulled up, but now I have twenty-three. Does anyone know where twenty-four is?"

Jewel wanted to raise her hand and say something, but what could she say? She didn't want to call attention to herself. Confessing twenty-four had vanished into the desert after a tryst in the shower, that wouldn't help anything. Her ears and whiskers dropped. Maybe last night was a bad idea.

Someone in the front of the bus spoke up, "Yeah, looks like he's coming."

Jewel turned. Running across the parking lot was Christian, carrying his suitcase. The bus driver went down the steps, and when the ocelot got close the bear grunted at Christian. "You are lucky I counted, son."

"Sorry," mumbled the ocelot as the bus driver took his suitcase, and he bounded up the steps. At the front of the bus he glanced around and spotted Jewel. He then walked down the aisle and took the seat next to her.

"I didn't think you were going to come back," whispered Jewel.

Christian sucked in his breath. "I had to think about last night. The walk helped me clear my mind."

"I'm sorry I pushed you into that. I got carried—"

A hand fell on hers as the bus driver came back up the stairs and closed the door. Jewel just waited for Christian to say something. The driver pulled off and honked at the repair guys who were looking over the other bus.

"I really did have to think," Christian said after a bit. "You make a cute girl."

Jewel nodded softly. "Thanks."

Christian squeezed Jewel's hand. "You make an even cuter guy though. I've got a confession to make."

The leopard sucked in a breath. "What?"

"I knew you were a guy before you told me. I didn't want you to know I knew."

"Really?" asked Jewel, loosening some of the feminine quality he tried to put into his voice when he had the dress on. "So you wanted to hook up with a guy anyway?"

The ocelot sighed. "Part of the reason I'm moving to Las Vegas is I know I need to get out of my old life and go find myself. Since I grew up in Oklahoma City, I was not going to get out my rut by staying there."

Jewel pressed the issue. "Like find yourself how?"

The other cat scratched behind his ears. "I'd been doing what felt easy. What I thought people expected of me. I had a girlfriend, but it wasn't as serious to me as it was to her. She was a nice girl, but she deserved someone who was into her. I realized I was just going through the motions with her. After we broke up I felt relieved."

"So you decided to explore?"

He nodded. "A little. I had a buddy who liked to watch porn and masturbate with friends, but the last time I went over there, I realized it wasn't the porn I was into. I also had this sucky construction job I was sticking with, so when I got a better opportunity in Vegas, I decided to take a chance."

"You've been taking a lot of chances," suggested Jewel, with a little growl in her voice.

"Apparently so!"

The leopard leaned in close, and whispered using his normal voice. "And you have a thing for being a 'pretty kitty', as you put it last night?"

Christian sucked in his breath and took the leopard's hand and squeezed it. "It appears," he said, blushing, "I do."

Jawell traced a hand toward Christian's crotch and brushed over it. Even now, the ocelot had a partial erection. "There's no harm in that. I do enjoy dressing as a woman, but I still know when a guy likes getting fucked. You, my friend, were in heaven there."

The ocelot shivered and nodded. "We'll have to do that again once we get to Nevada."

The leopard pulled back his hand and put both hands in his lap. "Oh really?"

"I mean if you are okay with that."

The leopard chuckled. "I don't know. With that toy, you're already on the way to loosening up. You might not need me."

"The real thing is so much better," whispered the ocelot, licking his lips. "Don't you want to help me explore the part of me I'm finally coming to terms with?"

Jewel could see in her mind what that would entail, and she liked what she saw. "Oh, I will," said the boy in the dress. "Oh, I will."

Loosening Up

"You need to loosen up," Leister told me, when I saw him two days ago. I wasn't sure exactly what he meant by that, but the fight that followed suggested it wasn't just about my ass. He thinks I'm too tense, I'm too prissy, I'm too whatever. Well, fuck him! Fuck him, fuck him, fuck him!

I screw my eyes shut and sigh. God, I wish he would have fucked me that night. I am just too tight, but for one of the tensions in my life, a good knot will fix that. I position my butt and lower it down so I can press the dog shaped dildo against my tailhole. At least one of those problems I know how to fix.

I just need to loosen up, I tell myself as I start to press the toy against my ass. I wish I knew other ways I could loosen up in my life.

"Oh, Leister, can't you just get it?" I whisper, as I feel the dildo sink into myself, the head slipping in. He loves me, and I love him, but things keep coming up between us, and they're not toys or knots.

Yes, I know I'm not perfect, but it isn't just me that is part of the problem. I growl in frustration and shove the dildo all the way! Fuck him—oh god that hurts!

My legs get weak due to the pain and I fall over onto my side, lying on my bed wincing, the toy buried in my ass.

"Muri, you idiot, you can't angry fuck yourself with a dildo." I growl to no one in particular.

My bedroom thankfully doesn't talk back, and I lie there panting. There is only a faint bit of Leister's African wild dog musk in here since he hasn't been over in a while, but my comforter still retains his scent. After a minute the pain calms down and I roll over onto my back, pull the toy out, and stare at it. Nine inches of slickened dog shaped black silicone looks back at me, ready to go back into one spotted hyena who, instead of taking the toy, is having a breakdown on his bed.

Maybe breakdown is the wrong term. I'm upset, but it will be okay, I think. I breathe out. I prepped myself for tonight just to end up dirty and unfucked on my own bed. I'm just too tense right now to do this.

"You need to loosen up," I can hear Leister saying to me in my head.

He's right, I do need to loosen up. Both if I'm going to take this toy right now and in general. I can't control everything. I can't help if I have to work late sometimes or he doesn't have the money to go out when I want to. I'm still mad as hell at Leister for what he said, but I can't say it's all him; my job has been stressful as hell lately.

"Okay, let's do this," I say, pushing myself up, and go back to kneeling on top of the towel on my bed. I grab the lube and squeeze some more onto my left paw, then I start fingering myself, gently teasing my hole with one digit and then a second. I'm careful with my probing not to scrape my claws against my sensitive insides. My cock gets hard again, finally coming back to attention.

If only this was Leister and not me. I pull my fingers out and grab the toy. I squirt a little more lube on it then reposition it under me. Slowly I lower myself to get it into the right spot. I can feel the tip pressed nicely against my ass, waiting for reentry. I wiggle my butt while holding the base down, letting it rub up and down the cleft of my cheeks. I've done this to Leister before, and it drives him crazy.

Finally, when I'm feeling in the mood again, I stop jiggling my butt and position myself. Slowly I sit down on the toy, letting the tip slip into me, feeling the head and then the tapered shaft below it. There, that's better. I'm feeling looser now that I've relaxed. I'm going to try and take this knot before I let myself cum. Working up and down the length above the knot, I remember the last time the two of us had sex. I bought this thing because of Leister. It's not always easy for me to take his knot, and I wanted to get better at doing that. I think it's helped me loosen up a lot already, and I enjoy anal more now.

I start stroking my shaft as I press down against the knot, feeling it press against the ring of muscle around my opening. "Oh, Leister, take me honey," I moan out. I pull up and push down against the toy, trying to force the thickest part of the silicone inside of me.

My phone starts ringing just as I'm getting the knot in and I yelp, surprised, shoving the whole thing in as I startle and sit down on the dildo.

"Argh!" I wince, and I have to bite my lip to keep from cursing. Who the fuck is calling me right now?

I grab the phone off my bed stand, not realizing I used the hand I lubed myself up with. The phone flies off the nightstand and lands on the bed face down. Grumbling, I have to scoot forward to get it. I'm just going to send them to voicemail and finish this. Finally, I get the phone in my non-slick paw and flip it over. I've got lube all over the case, but I'll clean it later. On the screen there is a picture of an African wild dog, a face of black, tan, and white fur smiling up at me. The name Leister is below the portrait.

I freeze. He hasn't talked to me since the fight except to tell me goodnight when I got home. In a moment of brilliance, I slid the call button to answer and hold the phone up to my ear, sitting back before I realize what's still in my butt.

"Heeeeyyyy…." I get out with a whine, trying to hide my discomfort.

"Hey," he says, a little confused. "Are you okay, Muri?"

I glance down at my hard dick. "I'm fine. How's you?"

"I was thinking about what happened, and I wanted to apologize," he says. "I'm sorry I called you uptight and stuff. I think you are a great guy, and I realize sometimes I'm just an asshole."

Lord, not this. Can't he just tell me he loves me? "It's fine."

"It is? You were really upset and—"

"It's fine," I hiss. "Just, I'm a little busy right now too," I add, my hand drifting down toward my shaft. I'm starting to go soft, and I'd like to finish what I started.

"Oh. I didn't know. I'll keep this brief then."

"Let me call you back tomorrow," I say.

"Tomorrow?" he says, confused.

I give myself a quick stroke. "Yes, tomorrow!"

He is taken back by that. "Sorry, I thought you'd be free right now."

"It's 10 o'clock on a Friday night, what do you think I'm doing?"

"Oh. Oh! Have fun."

God, he thinks I'm hooking up with someone. That's fine with our relationship agreement, but I don't do that anymore. "It's not that!" I blurt out.

"Okay…"

Ugh, no point in lying. "I've got a canine dildo up my ass and my dick in my hand, okay?"

Silence.

"Leister?"

"Yes, Muri?"

"You, uh, don't want to ask about that?"

He coughs. "I'm not sure what to ask exactly. Canine?"

"Yeah, remember I told you I bought one shaped like you?" I say, wiggling it in my ass. The knot stays nicely in place. "I even showed you. I think about you when I use it."

"When I told you to loosen up, I didn't mean like that."

"I know, you idiot, but that's what I'm doing right now!"

He clears his throat and then whispers. "Tell me how it feels."

"Filling. It's pretty wonderful."

"How so?" he asks me, drawing out the words.

I pull up off the knot with a gasp. "Well, for starters," I press down, slipping it back in, "it's much quieter than you are when I pop it in and out."

I get a squeaky laugh out of him. "You like the noises I make."

That's true for sure. I turn on speaker phone and set my cell phone down on the bed. "I do. Would you like to listen to me finish?"

"I can come over…"

I stroke along my shaft, pressing my ass down with the dildo into it. The bed creaks. "That will be too late."

He whines and I think I can hear fabric shuffling. "You can at least let me catch up."

"I'm still mad at you, so why should I?" I say, working my member back to attention.

"Because who is going to fuck you as good as I do?"

"That assumes I think you're good," I whine out. Getting close.

"In a van?"

"In a van?" I say pausing, hand over my dick.

"Yeah, I've been working on the van some more. I've got the kitchen set up finally. It's pretty slick. I was calling to see if you wanted to take the Transit out for a week next month."

A week alone with Leister in a camper van, just me, him, and the open road? "And what would we do," I say breathlessly.

"Anything you want, spotty boy. Hopefully I'll get to see how you've been loosening up."

That does it and I cum hard, shooting vigorously. I whine loudly. I get some of it on the towel, but a lot of it ends up on the comforter.

"I'm going to take that as a yes," he says, breathless. I can hear a stroking sound coming through the phone.

"Of course. You know I love your van, Leister."

"And me?" he pants.

"Absolutely," I say gingerly, sitting up and pulling the toy out carefully. I toss it onto the comforter. I'll just wash it all later.

"I love you too," he whispers back.

I lie on my side and reach behind me to probe at my tail-hole. It's still slick. If he was here, I could go again in a few minutes. "Tell me how much."

He lets out a chirping whine. "More then I love my van, that's for sure."

"It better be more than that van."

I can hear him just panting and then his breath catches, and he exhales. "It is."

I probe myself, feeling the muscles gently. "So, want to see how loose I'm getting tomorrow night?" I say with a giggle.

He laughs, high pitched and squeaky. "Sure."

I screw my eyes shut. "Your place, my place, or the van?"

"It's a little tight in the back, but we can do it in the van. Did you want to take it out to a campground?"

"There are some over in Pleasanton. If we call in the morning, we can find a place."

"I'll be by late morning then," he says. "I've got a few quick things to do before I come over."

"That's fine. It's last minute anyway."

"I've gotta go clean up, Muri," he says. "Have a good-night, and I'll see you in the morning."

"You too, Leister. I love you!"

There is just a brief pause, and then, "I love you too." The phone goes dead.

I reach over for the canine dildo on the bed and look at it. Maybe I can get a second round out of myself tonight. I think I'm going to try at least.

I wrote the first draft of this story back in 2017 at a writing retreat. One of the other participants at the retreat presented a story that had people living a van, but there wasn't any sex in the van. I decided to fix that, and that's how I ended up writing about Van Life. This was published in FANG Volume 10 *by FurPlanet back in 2019.*

Unknown Stains

Go to work. Go home. Go to sleep so you can get up in the morning and do the whole thing over again. Life is supposed to be fun. Life is supposed to be experienced. Life is supposed to be lived! Yes, I care about my job and my apartment and all the responsibilities in my life, but at the end of the day, there are only two things in this world I really care about. One of them I like to put in my mouth and ass. The other is the person attached to that object. Some might say my real priorities are questionable, but I just call them uncomplicated. It's at least the one thing in life that's easy to deal with.

Of course, in a moment like this, when I'm covered in dried mud, being dragged through the desert by the second thing, I kind of wish I had just the first to contend with right now.

"I thought the point of this trip was to enjoy ourselves," I snip, carefully walking through the arroyo we're crossing and the small amount of water at the bottom of it.

"Hey, you picked this trail," he calls from the top of the gully. "You shouldn't have fallen in on the way out to the mesa."

"I said we should plan a trip through the desert! Not through a lake!" I throw my hands up in the air.

He laughs. "It does occasionally still rain out here."

"You could have warned me, Leister!"

The painted dog gives a squeaky, high-pitched laugh. "I figured when I jumped over the water, you would have shown some caution, Muri. But we'll get you cleaned up. I'm an expert at doing that."

I growl back in response as I reach the top of the gully and we keep hiking across the scrub desert. "You're just jealous the stream got me and not you."

He chuckles. "Just don't sit on anything of value when we get back to the van."

"Yeah, yeah. The hyena is the dirty, unclean one. Like you never dribble."

He glances back at me, his black muzzle and tan face amused. "I'm not the one who decided to play connect the dots with his fur."

I just grumble and keep following his white-tipped tail down the trail. I'll get him back later, but at least the view of his butt is really good right now.

✍

There is something fun about road trips. You get to see a lot of places you've never been, and it's a great chance to relax. I have a very stressful job, but I can put that behind me at times like this. I can focus on just being me, not the me I have to be at work. I really enjoy these experiences, especially trips through the desert. Out here, you're free of some of the restrictions of daily life. There is just the sun, the sky, the feeling of freedom, and oh yeah, the gas station hose down.

"Would you stop fidgeting!" he yells at me.

The wind is blowing gently, across the open land. There are bushes nearby, but they don't offer much of a wind break.

"It's cold," I whine. Since its spring, the desert heat hasn't settled in yet.

He splashes the water onto my face. "Oh, come on, it's not that bad," he says with a snicker.

I growl. "I'm wet, I'm cold, and I'm standing in a gas station parking lot in my shorts."

He smiles. "If you don't let me hose all this mud off you, your fur is going to be sticky. Plus, the instruction manual says you should wash your hyena at least once a week."

I roll my eyes. I look ridiculous. "I will get you back for this."

He chirps, amused, and hangs the hose back up on the air and water kiosk. "Go change, yena," he says, pointing to the van, as he heads over to the convenience store.

I climb into the vehicle and close the sliding door behind me. Outside of the windows in the front, the Transit has a window in both rear doors and one in the sliding door. The ones in the back of the vehicle have special insulated covers I can pull down. I could close them, but they're tinted, and its bright outside. I do pull the curtain closed that separates the rear of the van from the cabin in the front to give myself some privacy. If someone comes to the back, they might notice I'm changing, but I don't care. You really shouldn't be looking into someone's vehicle anyway.

Leister bought the Transit used with low mileage and has adapted it into a camper van. The van has two seats in the front, then behind that is a small kitchenette across from the sliding door. You're not going to be cooking a big meal in it, but the kitchen is functional and has a fridge. The rest of the space is taken up by a queen-sized futon mattress in the back. The bed has some storage underneath it, and you can open the rear doors for a breathtaking view. The entire living space is paneled in wood to make it feel like a home. I helped him with some of the work, but most of this he did himself. The camper van is intimate, and that's what I like about it.

I have to be careful not to get any water or residual mud on the floor while I'm changing and tossing my clothing into a laundry bag. After peeling off my wet clothes off, I towel down before I fish out some fresh clothes from the long, narrow built-in cabinet over the bed that has my clothing. I only have a t-shirt on when Leister comes back and gets into the driver's seat of the van.

He pushes aside the curtain to glance back toward me. "How you doing back there?"

"Hey, some privacy you know!"

"Not like I haven't seen that before," he remarks, letting the curtain fall back. "I got you some coffee," he adds, and I can hear him putting something into one of the cup holders.

My ears perk at this. "Is it good?"

"It smells a little old, I'm afraid. It's all they had though."

I pull on a pair of boxers and walk over to push the curtain aside. I crawl into my chair and pick up the cup of coffee. "In moments like this, I'm reminded of how well you know me. There is nothing like a bad cup of stale, gas station coffee to get me moving and warm a yena's heart."

Leister turns on the van. "Two things. First, you're welcome. Second, have you thought about pants?"

I take a sip of the coffee. It is indeed stale, but it's sweetened and has creamer just the way I like it. "I have indeed thought about pants. They're in my clothing cubby."

He backs the van out of its parking space. "Are we giving the truckers a show now?"

"Maybe once we get off a two-lane road," I say.

"Oh, so this is an invitation?" he asks, as he pulls out of the gas station. The van bumps down the road out across the gently rolling hills.

I pull down my underwear to expose my sheath, which flops out. "Ready, willing, and able."

He glances over at me. "Ready, willing, and able to get arrested by the highway patrol."

"Hey, it's a new meaning to the term jailbait," I say.

He laughs. "Jerk."

My ears fall a little. "You don't want to get arrested?"

He glances at me. "What bad porno have you been watching that ever gave you the idea that is a good experience?"

I blush. "It wasn't—okay it was really bad."

He giggles and we fall silent as he drives down the road. When we're together like this, we're close. But when we're apart, we lose this closeness. Maybe it's us, or maybe it's just life getting in the way. My work can suck up a lot of my life. Maybe now is the time to finally ask him the question that's floating around in the back of my mind.

I appreciate nice things. They're pretty, and I like pretty, but I also like it when things are simple and uncomplicated; so, while the mattress in the back of the van isn't super thick, I don't mind that we're sleeping on it. I'm at home in this vehicle a way that surprises me. Leister's been working on this camper van conversion for a while, and I'm glad I got to help him. In this vehicle, we're free in a way I never experienced before. I still have my life and my apartment, but for a week, it's just us and the open road.

We decide to camp tonight off a dirt road that connects to a remote highway. It's a quiet spot next to small spring, and we leave the back door of the van open so we can see the water. Grass and brush grow right along the small pool's edge that gives way to scrub desert. We build a small fire from dead brush we collected so we can make our little campsite homey. We're not the first people to do this either; there's a small circle of stones with ashes in it we use. I also run out a temporary clothesline so I can dry my clothing.

Now watching the sky darken and the stars come out, I feel at peace with the world. I like being with the painted dog, out here alone in the desert. Lying on the bed in the van, I would be remiss to say I don't have expectations of what will happen tonight either. I never did put on any pants, so the night air is cool against my fur. Leister took his shirt off a while ago.

"It's so peaceful out here," Leister remarks, taking a sip of a beer he fished out of the fridge earlier.

"Yeah, it is. I'm glad we could plan this trip."

"Yeah. It was a great idea of yours."

I chuckle and wag my tail, watching the fire. "Thanks."

"I'm a little surprised you didn't want to invite anyone else," he says.

"And waste this moment?"

He laughs, trailing a paw through the fur on my arm. "Is that what this is? I mean you still have your underwear on and all."

My ears flatten. "No need to rush it."

"I guess not." He finishes his beer and tosses the can onto the ground outside.

"Really, littering?"

"Really, turning me down for sex?" he retorts.

"I didn't turn you down!"

"Well, I didn't litter either. It's only litter if I don't pick it up before we leave. Plus, do you want to roll over in the middle of fucking and get a can in your back?" He smiles at me, his amber eyes shining when they catch the light of the fire.

"You'll still forget."

"I may be an asshole, but I'm not that kind of asshole."

I chuckle. "You aren't an asshole, Leister."

"Okay how about uncouth, blunt jerk?"

I prop myself up on one arm. "Maybe."

"Oh, come on. You don't need to be kind on my account."

"Fine. Uncouth asshole?"

He slaps me on the shoulder, and his tail wags. "Yup." He lies down on the futon.

I roll my eyes. We do this dance all the time. He's told me before I should find someone better, but I don't want to. I want Leister, and that's what I'm working to get.

"Hey, why do you always put yourself down like this? You're not a bad guy."

He shrugs. "Dunno. I just do."

"You say you're an uncouth asshole, but you'd be the first to offer his seat on a bus to someone who needs it."

He gives me a squeaky laugh. "There is a difference between being impolite and being uncouth."

"Yes, but… I love you."

An arm wraps around my shoulder. "I love you too."

I whine. He's not getting it, and I'm up against his emotional defenses I don't feel I ever can quite break through. Now would be the time to try. "I love you, a lot. Like, I was thinking about asking if you wanted to move in."

He turns to look at me, ears up in surprise. "Move in?"

"Yeah, move in. We're obviously compatible. If we can live out of a van for a week, we can live together."

"I guess? I'm kind of a slob you know. I'm not sure I really quantify as roommate material."

"I think you do. You're not pretentious, and you're very grounded. I love that about you. Plus, we've been together long enough, haven't we? Why not move in."

He sighs. "I dunno, Muri. I thought this was more a thing of convenience. You told me when we started you wanted to keep it open."

"You know I'm not playing around on the side anymore."

His ears lower and he looks away. "Yeah, I know."

"Are you?"

He sighs. "Occasionally, but it's not anyone new though. It's been a few months since the last time I did. I know it bothers you if I do."

I sit up. "I have to ask this, and I'm serious about this. Do you want to keep it open?"

Leister frowns. "It's not a simple yes or no answer. It's less about sexual needs and more like, why me?"

"You're a great guy."

He sighs, and his ears fall. "I worry I'm not though."

"Dude, remember last year when I went skiing last minute by myself?" I say.

"Yeah. You fell."

"Breaking your leg is bit more than falling." Leister also has the decency not to remind me that I didn't fall on the ski slope but I slipped on ice in the parking lot of a restaurant after a great day of skiing.

He grins. "Okay, a bit more than falling."

"Yeah, but you took the bus to South Lake Tahoe and drove me home in my car after I got out of the hospital. You didn't have to do that for me. Hell, no one else was going to come get me, but you, you did that. Jerks don't do that for someone else. Good guys do that for people."

He doesn't say anything at first. "I guess, but I thought we just agreed on 'uncouth asshole' instead of 'good guy.'"

I look at him, searching his face. "I mean that jokingly. You're too nice to be a real asshole."

He gets up and moves over to the edge of the van door, so he can hang his feet off the end of the bed. "I'm not sure if this makes sense, but I don't want to disappoint you, Muri."

"Disappoint me? How would you disappoint me?"

The painted back shrugs. "Don't know."

"Leister, who else knows you better than me?"

He tilts his head to glance back. "Not sure anyone else does."

"Then if I think you're a great guy, why can't you accept that?"

"Because I worry you can find someone else."

I push myself over to the edge of the bed so I can wrap my arms around him. "What if I don't want to?"

He lets his shoulders slump and he kicks his feet. The bed sits on top of a raised platform in the back of the van. It's too high for Leister's feet to reach the ground, so they swing back and forth. "I try and hold down the fears I have inside about myself."

"That you'll hurt me?"

"Maybe that. Maybe I'm holding you back. When we started I didn't want to get serious. I enjoyed having someone who was just into me. Now…now I know it's not just that."

I lick one of his ears and shift my hand through his chest fur. "The possibility of us having more sex is not why I want you to move in. I think we've reached that stage. The last three years have been great. It's had its ups and downs, but I think we're good together."

"Has it been three years?"

"Yup," I remark, reaching down toward his belly button. "Three wonderful years."

He murmurs an agreement and then leans back against me. I play with his stomach fur for a while, before I go further, gently teasing him through the fabric. He lets out that squeaky, high pitched, chirping bark he does when he's happy.

I press myself a little further, teasing him through his jeans while I snuggle up against him. When I break off and lie back on the futon, I don't have to tell him what I want. He naturally comes over to me after stripping his pants off.

His musk in moments like this is pleasant, but it isn't as strong as mine. The van already smells of us since this is the second day of our weeklong trip, but I know after tonight, it's going to be marked by us.

My tail thumps against the mattress as he straddles me. Only the soft sounds of night and the sound of our breathing fills the air. In the firelight coming in from outside, he is a series of shadows, with bits of amber on top of his whites and tans. Leister is beautiful, and I love tracing my fingers along his complex fur variations. But right now, the red shaft in front of me is my focus.

I taste him carefully, enjoying the feeling of how he twitches at my touch. His musk is stronger than normal; we've both been out in the heat today, so I imagine mine is too. The sensation is still pleasant and warm, the flesh supple as I wash my tongue across it.

He lets out another squeaky bark, this time with need on top of it as I suckle at his cock. I can feel his black and white digits wrapping around my own shaft once he pulls back my underwear.

Getting me to attention also doesn't take any significant effort. We continue for a while with him sitting on top of me before he pulls back. Wordlessly we shift positions so we can sixty-nine, me on the bottom and him on the top.

The feeling of his wet nose against my sensitive flesh is beautiful. I'm between his legs, and I can only see the outline of his body as I take him back into my mouth. He also doesn't waste any time licking my cock, as he holds it between his fingers. His long tongue paints me in wet, warm drool, coaxing me on. The sensation is blissful, and I am happy. This is my world right now, and this is the only world I wish existed.

I have my nose buried into his balls when I get that telltale twitch, and he has to break off to pant. With a shudder he cums, and I taste him, salty and familiar.

He gives me some breathing room by pulling out, but the painted dog doesn't stop. He licks teasingly and jerks me off, and I quickly reach my own climax. There is something about a job well done that I find really hot, and he feels the same way. He's a giving lover, not someone who stops once they've gotten off themselves.

I splatter cum all over me, him, and the bed. When we're done, he rolls over to lie next to me, my head at one end of the mattress, his at the other.

Being in this van with Leister, that is nice. My life and work don't intrude. I can barely get a cell phone signal out here anyway. Instead, we're just together, experiencing the open road. Being with him is more satisfying than anyone else I've been with. I don't know why. Sex always puts me in a good mood, but just being around Leister, I feel complete. Perhaps tomorrow, if I can find where I put the lube I swear I packed, we can do some anal.

"Hey, Muri, can I ask you a question?"

"Yeah?"

"Do we have a cum rag?"

"Uh, not really."

"I've got some of you on the side of my face and chest."

"Hey, you can never say I didn't give you anything nice. If you give me a bit, I can even gave you a proper pearl necklace tonight." I giggle amused.

Even after Leister punches me in the side, I am still laughing.

৯

There is something about dawn that wakes me up early when I'm camping. The night air with its cool breeze begins to warm a little, and the subtle shift in air temperature rouses me as the rosy fingers of dawn are spreading across the desert.

At first the sun will brighten the sky, and deep shadows cover the ground. Then the sun breaks over the horizon, bathing what it touches with golden light, making the sand shimmer as it rises. Pockets of shadow can run for miles in the nooks and crannies of the hills until finally the sun climbs high enough to illuminate everything.

Even though we have the back doors of the van open, the space is still cloaked in shadow. I glance toward Leister, watching his back of splotched fur as he breathes steadily next to me, still oblivious to the coming morning. He's curled against the wall opposite from me wrapped around a pillow, but his tail is draped across my stomach. We're naked except for the sheet that covers us.

I prop my head up by putting one of my arms under it and sigh. I can't believe I finally asked if he wanted to move in. I've been wanting to, but it's been tough to reach this point. He didn't say yes though, and he let it drop when I let my emotions and needs run high. I guess that went as well as I could expect. I stare up at the wooden ceiling. What was I thinking?

"Stupid, just stupid," I mutter, dropping my other hand as a balled fist into the futon mattress. "Just stupid."

"Hey, don't pick on the mattress now. What did that mattress ever do to you?"

I yelp. "I thought you were asleep."

He rolls over and yawns, washing my face in hot breath. "I've been awake thinking." He opens his eyes to look at me.

"About what?" I ask.

"Just general stuff, like where my life is and where it's going."

"That's pretty serious for this time of day."

He yawns again and lets his tongue roll out. "It happens. I've got a lot on my mind."

"I'm sorry," I blurt out.

"For what?"

I lower my voice. "Last night."

"Oh, that."

"Yeah, that."

"It's no biggie," he says.

Maybe not to him, but it is a big deal to me. "You never said if you wanted to move in or not."

"I'd have to think about it."

"That's what you were really thinking about, isn't it?"

He reaches out to rest a paw on my nearest arm. "It's only the second full day of our trip. Can we perhaps deal with the heavy stuff a little later?"

I blink. "I mean, I guess, but I don't want it hanging over our heads."

"Then you shouldn't have asked. What were you expecting me to say?"

I huff at him. "Obviously more than you did."

"Muri, come on. You can't just expect me to move in with you. We've got separate lives."

"We have separate lives because you want us to. It doesn't have to be like this. We could be a couple. A real couple, Leister. One with a real life together."

He sighs. "And what about what I want? All I'm hearing is what you want."

I draw back. "You don't want this?"

He sits up. "Muri, you are a great guy. You deserve better."

My ears splay. "So you've told me."

"Look at yourself. You've got a good thing going with your job. You've got money in the bank and a nice place to yourself. Me? I live in a studio in a drafty industrial loft. My landlord keeps raising my rent to the point I'm going to have to look somewhere else to live. Part of why I've kept working on the van is because I may have to live in it someday."

"You want to live in this permanently?"

"No, but it would save me some money. Now that the sink and burner setup are installed, I can even cook in here. Plus, if I move into it, I can travel more. I don't have to stay in California."

"Leister, that's cool and all, but..."

"But what about us?"

"Yeah."

"I figure you'll find someone better."

I slam my fist against the bed. "Leister, you dense, stupid idiot! This isn't about finding someone better. This is about making what we have work better for us. What the hell am I going to do, turn on Paw Mingle or Barked and bam, instant long-term lover? It doesn't fucking work that way!"

The dog's ears go down. "If you tried—"

"Tried? Tried! Why the hell would I want to try?" I snarl. "You know what, forget this. Forget I asked." I push myself up, crawl off the bed, and snag my discarded underwear. "I'm going for a walk, and when I come back, I'll pretend this doesn't bother me so we can enjoy our little trip."

"Muri—"

"Shove it, Leister!" I yell, jumping out the side of the van. My paws connect with dirt and I storm off, leaving the dog alone.

❧

The desert is a harsh place, and fifteen minutes later, I realize just how stupid what I have done is. I stop to catch my breath in the shade of a scrub bush and after kicking the dirt a few times, I look around to get my bearings. In every direction is desert vegetation cut through with small rises. I didn't take a bearing or try to keep track of the vegetation I passed. I just stormed out here. I can see the distant mountains, but in which direction is the van? Even more concerning, will Leister still be there when I return?

He wouldn't just leave me out here, would he? I don't think so, but if I can storm off, why can't he? I look around to try and find my trail, but I kicked up enough dirt I can't be sure exactly from which direction I came.

"Shit." Unlike yesterday's hike, I don't even have any water. Even though it is still spring, once the sun reaches high into the sky, this could quickly turn dangerous.

"Okay, think, Muri. Your ancestors hunted on the savanna for their meals. You don't even have to chase anything down; you just have to return to where you came from. I just need my superior instincts to kick in."

I take a deep breath and look around on the ground carefully, but everything looks the same. The ground is too hard and doesn't take pawprints easily. I'm in the middle of the desert with no water and my only article of clothing is a pair of boxers.

"I'm going to die out here," I say to the ground, as I fall to my knees. Nothing responds to me, and the insects that sing about the heat of the day don't respond to my sobbing. I'm completely alone right now, and I've taken some of the best time I've had with Leister and ruined it. I had to press him on moving in. I couldn't let it be. My desire to ask him has been eating at me for a while. I thought we were ready to take this step, but I apparently want more than he's ready to give.

Crying into the dust is probably not the best way to try and conserve water, but I do it anyway. I have so much emotion inside it just all comes tumbling out. I look absolutely ridiculous, a full-grown hyena crying in the middle of nowhere, wearing only a pair of underwear, with my head pressed against the ground.

If I don't know where I came from, does Leister know how to find me?

Big wet tears sink into the dirt, and eventually I run out of them. I am just dry heaving. I've fucked up my vacation with Leister, maybe even our relationship, and now I'm lost in the desert. If I don't come back, what is he going to think? What is he going to do?

That last question I know the answer to. He'll look for me. He isn't going to leave me out here. He knows how dangerous that would be, and he would never do that to me, no matter how mad he is at me.

I look up at the blue sky. We turned off on a side road to get to our camping spot south of the main road. The sun is still low in the east. If I start off north and use the distant mountains to keep me on a straight line, I should intersect the main road. From there, I might be able to walk back to the van, or at least hitch a ride with a passing vehicle. I might even be able to borrow someone's cell phone, although I don't know if Leister has service out here.

Or I could head toward that distant plume of smoke in the distance. I blink. Wait, if there is a campfire, that means someone is out here. That might even be Leister. We didn't use all the brush we collected last night.

I take a bearing so I know which way north is, and then I take off in a trot. Whoever it is, they can't be that far away. I hope they like mostly naked hyena. Nothing looks familiar, but in my anger, I saw without seeing.

A quick ten minutes later, I emerge out into the clearing we camped at. The van is still there and Leister is crouched over a fire. His ears are down, and he's focusing on his cast iron skillet that sits on top of a small metal grate propped up on the rocks around the fire.

"Leister!"

The wild dog startles and his ears shoot up. "Muri!" He stands up, a metal spatula clutched in one hand. "I started making breakfast. I thought you might want to eat."

I've noticed when he gets stressed out Leister cooks. It gives him something to do, and it's one of the tells he has. "You weren't going to come look for me, were you?"

"I figured you wanted your space." He looks down at the food sizzling in the pan. "You've got good timing though. The bacon is almost done."

"I uh, got lost," I say sheepishly.

He startles. "What?"

"Yeah," I say, tail between my legs. With nothing else to say for myself, I walk over to the van. I look ridiculous out here in my underwear. I should at least put some pants on finally.

As I walk past him, he reaches over and puts a hand on my shoulder to stop me. The spatula is clutched in his other hand. "I'm sorry. I didn't mean to upset you. I certainly didn't want you to go storming off like that."

"Well, you did."

Leister's ears twitch and lower. "Sorry. I get nervous about stuff like this."

That's something, I guess. "Yeah, it's a big change."

He steps forward and pulls me into a hug. "And please don't do that again. I don't want to have to call the police to comb through the desert looking for a hyena in a pair of boxers."

I chuckle. "It would be quite a story."

"Yeah, but not a good one," he says. He holds me for a minute and then breaks off the hug. He walks back over to the fire and pokes at the bacon in the cast iron skillet with the spatula. "How do you want your eggs?"

"Uh, scrambled, and wait, where did you get this food from?"

"From the fridge. Remember, I said I packed food? I wanted to surprise you with breakfast." He motions to a camp chair near the fire. "Give me a few minutes and it will be ready."

"Maybe I should get some shorts."

"Up to you. You be as naked or not as you want to be."

"I'm sorry about running off."

He pulls the bacon off the fire and puts it on a plate. He then wipes out some of the grease. "You have a right to be upset." He puts the pan back on the fire and starts to crack eggs into it.

"Yeah, but I have no right to force you into a relationship."

"We're already in a relationship."

I wring my hands. "Right, but something more serious."

He nods and keep cooking, ears focused on the sizzling grease and eggs. "If it helps put your mind at ease right now," he offers after a minute, looking up, "I wouldn't want to be out here with anyone else I know."

"Thanks."

"I mean really, I've got the best view out here."

"The spring is pretty nice."

"That's the second best view out here. I'm talking about you."

I smile. "Leister, that's kind of sweet."

"Now if only there wasn't underwear blocking it."

"Hey!"

He grins and gives me a squeaky laugh.

I chuckle and push my boxers down. "Better?"

The dog wags his tail. "Yeah," he says, going back to tend the eggs. "I'm looking forward to a morning swim after breakfast with that view, but first, can you get the plates out?"

"Sure," I respond, and walk over to the van to pull things out of the cupboard.

If there is one thing I have learned in my life, it's to let go of as many of the burdens holding you back as you can. The reason we took this trip is to live in the moment. To just be us. Yet here I've ruined that. Leister's cooking is good, but I've killed the lighthearted banter we normally have. We talk, but he seems pensive. I can tell he's thinking. Afterward, while I'm still poking at my food, Leister goes to make the bed.

"The two people who slept here are a real mess," says the dog, looking over the sheets.

"Sorry," I mumble, chewing on my last piece of bacon.

"I mean look at this," he says motioning me over.

"We weren't that messy, were we?" I walk over and look at the sheets. There is a dried milk white stain in the middle of the light green sheets. There are also some reddish-brown stains on the far end of the bed.

"Do you know how hard it is to clean cum out of a futon mattress?" the painted dog asks me, looking over the product of last night's love making. "And what are those?"

"If you can clean a hyena up at a gas station, I'm pretty sure you can hose down a mattress at one too."

"It wouldn't dry," he says. "Plus, I hosed you down yesterday and we still have weird mud stains on the bed. Maybe we can find a laundromat in the next town and do some washing over lunch."

The red stains do suspiciously look like mud from yesterday's dip in the arroyo. "Look, I don't know how they got there."

He glances at me. "Can you go inside and help me take this off?

"Sure," I say, going around to the side door and getting in. Leister passes me the pillows and I toss them into the seats up front. We pull off the sheets, which I toss in our shared laundry bag while he pulls out a spare set from storage area under the bed. Together we put the clean sheets on the mattress. While I'm putting the pillows back, he comes inside and sits down on the bed. There is a serious look in his face.

"Now you want to talk?" I ask him.

"Yeah."

I sigh and sit down next to him. He rests one of his paws on top of mine and we intertwine fingers.

"Muri?"

"Yeah?"

"What do you want for us?" he asks me.

"Something more serious than we have now. It's why I asked if you wanted to move in."

"You deserve better."

I roll my eyes.

"No, I mean from me. I've been thinking we could just continue as it is, but you want more. And if I want you, I have to realize that."

I nod. "I keep hoping you will, but I realize commitment isn't for everyone."

"I know and you're right. It's time to make that go."

"You aren't saying this just to make me feel better, are you?"

"No. I've known for a while you wanted to get more serious. Change isn't easy though. You keep a tight ship in your house, and me? Well I'm just kind of a free spirit who doesn't want to think too hard about where they're going in life. The future scares me, and a lot of time, I'm just trying to get through the day."

I squeeze his hand since I'm still holding it. "That's one of the things about you I appreciate though. You aren't pretentious about stuff. You just live. Me? I've got things always going on. I have to organize myself in order to be able to function."

"Yeah, I understand that. I wish I could be more like you sometimes, but I always liked to play it loose. Sadly, the world seems to want more you's than me's."

"Being me is tiring sometimes," I say. "It's what I love about these trips. Out here, we aren't playing our roles in society. Everything else just falls away. We're just living."

He sighs. "The right answer is probably somewhere in the middle."

"Yeah." I lean over and give him a kiss. "I'm glad you're willing to give living together a try."

His ears shoot up and his black muzzle beams, "It will take some getting used to, but I'm excited for it."

We fall silent, and he leans over so he can rest his head on my shoulder. He tilts his head up so he can give the side of my muzzle a lick.

After a minute, his tail starts thumping against the bed, and he gives me a squeaky bark. "Hey, I have an idea."

"What's that?" I ask.

"How about we just live out of the van?"

"Hell no! Do you see how hard it is to keep this futon clean?"

"Okay, your place is fine, but I mean really, what more could you want out of your life than what is in this van right now?"

Even though I know he's not serious about living in the van full-time, he makes a good point. As long as the two most important things in my life are here, I'll be fine. Yeah, we don't have a TV or anything like that, but my priorities are simple. At least the ones I want to focus on are simple. I mean really, what's not to love about this setup? Plus, what the hell else are we going to do at night besides fuck if we lived in the van?

Okay, we can't do that all the time, but it's nice to think we could. Yeah, I have other friends, a job with deadlines and commitments, and bills that need to get paid, but the basics of my life, the life I want to have, are here.

"With you in this van? Nothing."

Originally posted online in 2014, The Fluffer *is the oldest story in this collection. It deals with the unglamorous aspects of the porn industry, and leaves nothing on the table. It gets a little kinky, but it's all good fun in the end.*

The Fluffer

The salty taste of the cock in his mouth told Max that the wolf he was going down on had been working up a sweat. It was pleasant enough though, and he lapped at it eagerly with gusto, taking the shaft deep into his throat. It was thick and—with a few deft licks by Max—already hardening nicely in his mouth. Max closed his eyes to savor the taste and the moment, but it ended far sooner than he would have preferred.

The wolf pulled out of Max's mouth with a groan. "That's gonna do it, hun. Gotta have something for the scene, you know." Max smiled up at the wolf weakly. The wolf scratched behind Max's ears as one would pet a feral animal, before shooing him out of the way.

The raccoon sighed silently to himself, disappointed. He got up with a half-realized hard-on and the salty taste of Joshua's cock in his mouth. On the other side of the bed, there was an otter tied up. Max went over to him and pulled a bottle of lube out of his pocket to squirt some onto the otter's erect cock, quickly slickening the hardened length. He then stepped away from the bed, to take a swig on his water bottle and wash the taste of cock out of his muzzle.

"All right, let's get this shot going and finish up this scene," the weasel director said, as he stepped up to the bed.

Max drifted away from the bed while the director barked orders to the cameramen and the actors. Then there was the telltale snap of the clapperboard, and they started filming the scene. The moaning and the creaking on the bed began immediately, and that only made Max want to tear the fur off his head.

With apprehension, he turned around to watch. Joshua was banging the otter on the bed while the director motioned for one of the cameras to zoom in on the action. Joshua roughly gripped the otter's cock as he fucked him, jerking him along. Max could feel a tightness in his chest as he wished he could change places with either of the actors. He wanted to look away, but he couldn't. This was exactly what he wanted, but he was just on the sidelines. If he couldn't get his jealousy under control, he was going to have to find another job.

The sex went on for thirty seconds, and then Joshua pulled out so he could cum on the otter. As he pulled out, he shifted his weight so the camera could get a better angle. With a grunt, he came, shooting thick ropes of cum onto the otter. When he finished climaxing, the wolf sat back on the bed as the director shouted, "Cut!"

The stage sprung to life as everyone started moving about.

"That's exactly what we want in this film," said the director, coming up to pat Joshua on the back.

"Thanks," said Joshua, grinning up at the director.

"Mmph," was all the otter could manage.

"Max, get Carson untied," the director said, as he walked away from the bed.

Max walked over to the otter and started to undo the ropes. Carson looked up at him and mumbled something that sounded like a thank-you. As soon as Max loosened the ropes, Carson's body relaxed and he rubbed his wrists before he reached up to undo the ball gag.

"Gah," sputtered Carson with a dry, hacking sound. Max held up the water bottle and squirted water into Carson's muzzle. The otter licked his lips and then spoke. His voice was still dry. "Thank you," he said. "It feels like I've had sandpaper in my mouth."

"No problem," said Max. He was preparing to undo Carson's ankles when the director started shouting.

"If camera #2 was out of position, why didn't you say something?"

"I thought Joshua was going to use a different angle," the besieged cheetah cameraman offered.

The director sighed, his thin tail flicking back and forth. "Everyone, back to your places; we need to reshoot the end of the scene. Max, get Carson cleaned up. Then take Joshua and get him prepped up again."

Carson cursed something fierce. Max felt his chest fall. They'd already shot this scene once earlier today, and they were going to have to redo it again.

"I swear, I am never doing a fucking ball gag scene again. This is ridiculous," muttered Carson to the raccoon as he started to sponge down his fur.

Max looked over at Joshua. "At least you get something."

Carson rolled his eyes and scratched behind his ears. "If you think what they're paying me makes up for the sore ass, you are so mistaken."

ჽ

Raccoons had never been popular porn stars, but Max hadn't gotten into the adult film industry looking to score a role. He'd done a few scenes, but mostly he worked in the background prepping the actors. The fluffer role got him a chance to sample the most amazing cocks in the industry, but when it came to something more substantial, he was out in the cold.

The waitress at his favorite sushi place dropped off his sake bomb, and he gingerly slid it in front of himself. Joshua Swanks was his current favorite star to work with. He was big right now, and his movies were on top of the industry. When he wasn't busy filming, he was putting in appearances to build his reputation. Max slammed his fist silently on the table, forgoing the traditional shout. The shot glass of sake dropped into the beer with a clunk, causing the beverage to fizz. He then grabbed the glass and threw it back, letting the drink pour into his muzzle. He fantasized about the wolf a lot, but he knew he had about as much chance with Joshua as he had winning the lottery.

He put the glass down after gulping the contents. A lot of guys would love to get Joshua Swanks' cock in their mouth. He just wished he could actually get him in his mouth for more than thirty seconds. Hell, he wished he could get anyone inside his mouth for more than thirty seconds. He sighed. This is what his life had come to: sucking soft cocks and getting drunk alone in restaurants. He put his head on his paws. Maybe he should consider doing something else with his life, like finding a job in regular Hollywood. At least he wouldn't be teasing himself by going to work.

The vulpine sushi chef walked over to where Max was sitting at the sushi bar and put his order down in front of him. "Your usual, a spider roll and nigiri."

"Thanks," said Max, picking up the chopsticks and reaching for the soy sauce. He didn't have much of appetite, but he was going to force himself to eat. He needed food in his system.

"Hey, I didn't know raccoons liked sushi!"

Max jolted up and turned to his right. The ball-gagged otter who Joshua had been banging earlier in the week had appeared next to him.

"Everyone on the west coast likes sushi," said Max, surprised.

"True enough," said the otter, sliding into a seat next to Max.

The raccoon tensed a little. He didn't want company right now, and while he knew Carson, he only really knew what his cock was shaped like. Max had worked on some films where the otter had bottom roles against power tops. He'd fluffed him a few times, but they had never talked off set.

"It's good I ran into you," the otter said, a smile on his muzzle. "I'm working with a new director, and he's short on staff. We're looking to do some shooting next week. Are you available?"

"Uhh," said Max, going over his mental calendar. "Only after Wednesday."

"Oh, cool. The film is called, 'An Otter on the Serengeti.' I'll talk to the director and have him call you. This will be my first starring role! I get to slut it up with some big cats this time. There is even some real dialogue to this one, so I get to actually act."

"That's nice," said the raccoon, picking at his sushi.

The otter squinted at the raccoon. "You look a little off; are you okay?"

Max looked at him. The otter's ears were pointed toward Max. "It's just been a long day."

"I understand that. Hey, before I forget, what's your number?"

"Huh? Oh, for the director?"

"Yeah," said Carson pulling out his phone and handing it to Max.

Max silently took the phone, tapped in his number, and handed it back to Carson.

"Thanks." The otter hopped off of the bar stool. "I have some friends I'm here with, but I'll hopefully be seeing you next week."

Max sighed and watched the otter walk off. He joined a crowd of guys at a big booth. One of them, a bear, wrapped his arm around Carson. Max recognized a few of the people; he knew them from various films he'd worked on or seen, and at least two he'd had to prep for scenes.

The raccoon turned back to his food. He reached for the empty sake bomb, but put it down when he realized there was nothing left in it. He was going to need another drink.

৶

The film Carson had gotten involved with was a rather low budget affair. The director had rented a sound stage in a building that felt more like an oven than a movie studio. The constant stale air gave off a dry heat that made the studio stifling. This produced a strong musk on set that didn't just come from the actors.

As for the dialogue, it was so hokey it made Max wish he hadn't gotten into this production. Carson, though, seemed to love it. Of course, being the star in any adult film was a step up from being a stock bottom. Even if the otter had to take a lot of cock, he was the star of the show, and you could tell he enjoyed the attention.

Still, it did pay, and the work was what he usually did. Fluff, watch, repeat. He'd get the cats at attention, and then Carson would lick on camera until they came. At the end of the day, go home by yourself alone.

Max was certainly becoming familiar with Carson's package. He could easily recall the curve of it in his muzzle, but the person behind it, that was still a mystery to him. He was definitely a sexy mystery, and Max wondered what types of moans and squeaks he could get out of the otter given the chance. That was the part of the work he enjoyed, and even though he never got to finish the blowjob or handjob he started, he at least got to touch the merchandise.

He shook himself out of his daydreams. The director had already left for the day, and after he finished breaking down this sling, he was out of here too. Only a few of the camera men were still milling about, cleaning the camera equipment.

"Hey, Max!" came a call. It was Carson, and that made his tail go stiff. He'd thought all of the actors had already left for the day to go out for drinks together to celebrate the first week of shooting being done.

"Yeah," said Max, turning around.

"You need a hand with that?" asked the otter, kneeling down to help.

Max didn't know how to answer that. The otter didn't have to help him, so why had he decided to now? "Sure," he said after hesitating.

The otter started to undo the other arm of the sling that Max was currently unbolting. Carson already had his street clothes on, but he wasn't wearing anything fancy. "So, I've been meaning to ask you. What do you think of the movie?"

The raccoon paused and looked over at Carson. He was usually pretty tactful about his opinions, but he was tired and sore tonight. Carson looked eager to hear what he said, and there was a certain honest interest in his expression that caused Max not to sidestep his feelings about the film.

"I'm sorry, but I think it's one of the lowest quality films I've worked on that wasn't filmed at someone's house."

The otter flicked his ears back and his muzzle hung open a little.

"And honestly," said Max going on, "the dialogue sucks. It would have been better as a straight porno without any attempts at conversation."

Carson closed his muzzle. "I guess that means you don't like it."

"Pretty much," said Max, as he disconnected the leather harness and started to fold it up.

Carson sighed. "You know this is my big break into a leading role?"

Max looked at the otter. "Well, what do you think of it?"

Carson looked around, then smiled. "The dialogue does suck, the studio is cheap, and the director is a two-bit hack. It is one of the few films I've seen that wanted a starting otter, so I'm hoping it will at least sell."

Max didn't say anything. He just took the metal bracket Carson handed to him and set it down on the flatbed dolly he was loading the swing onto.

"When I graduated from acting school, this wasn't exactly what I had in mind, but it's something," said the otter.

"You went to school for this?"

"Yup," the otter said, blushing. "Now I get banged by big cats hoping to make it to something better. It's not exactly glamorous work, but it is work. Hey, you want to go grab some sushi tonight?"

Max paused and looked up at the otter. That wasn't something he had been expecting. "Uhh, with your friends?"

"Oh, those guys?" laughed the otter. "They're a bunch of horn dogs. Not only do they make porn for a living, they try to live in a porn. We were out celebrating my new film that time, so I wasn't going to turn down the opportunity to network with them. No, this would just be you and me."

Max nodded. At least he wouldn't have to be alone tonight. "Sure, it's not like I have any other plans for tonight."

ço

"So," said Carson as he poured hot sake and then slid the small cup over to Max, "how did you get into the adult film industry?"

The low lighting was relaxing, and he was enjoying the soft music playing in the background. Max might have felt embarrassed to answer it, but the secluded booth in the back of the restaurant was private enough he didn't think they would be overheard.

"It just kind of happened. I got an opportunity to meet some porn stars, and it spiraled from there. I did some minor roles and then ended up working behind the scenes." Max took the offered cup of sake and sniffed it before taking a sip. The sake was sweet with hints of fruit to it.

Carson nodded. "Do you find it fun?"

Max blushed a little, thinking back to when he'd had Carson in his muzzle earlier in the day and the small squeak he'd given off when he was ready for the scene and Max needed to stop. "Sometimes."

Carson smirked and leaned forward. "You like the guys, huh?"

Max blushed deeper. "And you don't?"

The otter shrugged and sipped his sake. "I used to. Most of them are kind of airheads."

"So why are you in the business?" asked Max.

"I keep hoping that someday, I'll get a break and a role that will get me out of this and start me on the road to being a real actor. Mostly I just lie there, take it, and moan. It's easy money for a starving actor."

"Well, you do it well."

"Yeah, but I'm typecast," said the otter. "I feel I'm pretty flexible in bed, but being an otter, I only get submissive roles. Even with this movie, I'm playing the sub. Don't get me wrong now, there are more big name bottoms than tops, but I would like to get the chance to actually top on film." Max took another sip of his sake. "I guess at this rate, all I can hope for is to be the next Ty Ruddertail. Now that's an otter who has a sweet ass."

"Raccoons don't get a lot of respect in this business either. The few times I ended up in front of the camera, all I did was sit there and suck some cock in the background of an orgy scene. Most people don't think we're very sexy, and they think we're too chubby to be in front of the camera."

Carson smiled. "I find you sexy. I mean, you're no Ty Ruddertail, but you're not a career 'pool boy' like he is." The otter winked. "Also, you do suck a mean cock."

Max blushed, his ears taking on a reddish tinge.

"Now don't do that," said the otter, noticing Max's deep blush. "Remember, I'm stuck being the proverbial cock warmer. It's nothing to be ashamed of."

Max just finished off the rest of his sake and put the cup down. Carson poured him some more.

"I confess, this isn't exactly a normal conversation. Here we are talking about sex so casually like it's nothing," the otter mused.

"That bothers you?" asked the raccoon.

"Doesn't it bother you? We're surrounded by so much sex at work; it's lost its meaning."

Their waiter arrived then with their food and set down two plates of sushi. Max picked up his chopsticks.

"You mean there is no passion to it, and it has become mechanical?" Max asked Carson.

"Yeah, there is no love," said the otter, popping a piece of fish into his muzzle before he even poured himself some soy sauce. He closed his eyes to chew and savor the flavor.

"It looked like you enjoyed that scene with Joshua, and you were really moaning today in that sling."

The otter smirked. "I'm paid to moan like that for a living."

"Yeah, but you get to brag now that you've slept with Joshua Swanks."

"Hey now, I've never slept with Joshua," Carson said, pointing a chopstick at Max. "Well, okay, I've slept with him, but not off camera. On camera, you perform. It has all the motions of the real feel, the same sensations, but when it's done, you go clean up and that's it. Joshua is nice to look at, but he wouldn't do it for me. I need something more than a hot lay, I need something up here," the otter said, tapping his head. "Based on your definition of 'sleeping together', you've blown a lot of different guys."

Now it was Max's turn to get defensive. "None of them ever finished."

"So?" smirked the otter.

They ate in silence for a few minutes, savoring the sushi. Sushi hadn't originally been Max's thing, but he'd developed a taste for it living on the west coast. The salmon was rich, and the sauce on his sushi roll made his tongue tingle. Carson's tail wiggled back and forth as he ate, showing his deep contentment.

"I think you're right about how desensitizing to sex this work is," said Max. "I've stopped even thinking about dating anyone. Hooking up is where the action is, and that's all I think I will ever find. I can't even seem to do that well anymore either. Have you dated anyone seriously since you got into the business?"

Carson shook his head. "I've hooked up with a few other stars, but mostly the sex tends to be mechanical. It's hot, but when it's over, it's over; they want to kick you out of their house then. I feel like a hopeless romantic when I say I just want to snuggle with someone."

Max sat back and appraised the otter. He'd always been into the big stars—the guys who had the big tools or showed off the nicest bodies. Carson was buff, but he wasn't a muscle head. His thick, stiff fur didn't give him great muscle definition. He could feel the stirrings of something he hadn't thought about in a long time. He put down his chopsticks and leaned forward to take one of the otter's hands.

"Don't let what you do take away what will make you happy." He wasn't sure if this was for his benefit or Carson's, but it was what came to him.

Carson's eyes widened, but he smiled. "You're right. I'm just doing this until I can do better. If I keep working hard, I'll get a real acting gig."

"Exactly," said Max, going over his own working situation in his head. Maybe he could land a job as a rigger or a camera operator on a normal production. He'd filled in on both spots in the adult industry, so he had the experience.

"You know what, I think I'm going to talk to the director tomorrow and see if we can't improve some of the dialogue. I've got a few ideas on ways to make it better. I doubt he'd want to reshoot anything, but perhaps the movie can be improved a little."

"Ahh, now you're thinking outside of the box," said the raccoon.

"Exactly," said Carson, his thick tail thumping. Their eyes met and Max couldn't tell if Carson was really into him, or just wanted someone to talk to. There was a connection there for a moment, and then Carson broke it off to pop another piece of sushi in his mouth.

The rest of dinner was small talk and swapping stories about different actors. That night, when he was asleep in his bed, Max didn't dream about Joshua Swanks. Instead of the hunky wolf, there was an otter with a penchant for sushi and sake.

℘

Max pulled up at work Monday morning a little early. Every production he worked on was different, so he never knew what to expect. The sun was up, but the parking lot seemed a little emptier than usual. Still, he was early; it wasn't until he entered the studio that he realized something was wrong. The lights over the stage were off, and everyone present was milling about near the entrance talking.

"Hey," he said to the group of crew members, "what's going on?"

A swift fox who'd worked in the industry for twenty years spoke up. "The movie is off. The director showed some of the footage to his backers, and they didn't like it. They're pulling the plug on the movie. I think they wanted something more upmarket."

"What?" said Max. "We haven't even been paid for the last week of work."

"Yeah, well, the director said the studio would cover us for that, but that's it. They're asking for a few people to help break down the set, and clear out. The rest of us can go home."

Max shook his head. He'd never had this happen before. He'd turned down working on a small production next week just a few days ago since this movie was supposed to shoot for four weeks and they were just one week in.

"Well, if they're paying for breakdown, I'm in," he said.

"I didn't think you could create a porno so bad it would get canceled while filming," said one of the cameramen.

"Go figure," said the swift fox. "There are lows even the adult industry won't stoop to."

As the crew talked, Carson came out from the back of the studio. He looked very upset, and Max tried to flag him down.

"Carson!" said Max, breaking away from the crowd and heading over to intercept him.

"Yeah," the otter said tiredly when the raccoon walked up to him. He'd been crying, and his eyes looked puffy.

"You okay?" asked Max.

The otter sniffed. "My first starring role as a lead, and the entire movie gets canned."

"Hopefully this is just a bump in the road for you. You got any other work lined up?" Max asked.

"No," he sighed. "I'll call my agent and see, but it will probably be some other dumb orgy flick. Even as an adult actor, I can't get into the good productions."

Max wrapped an arm around the otter to try and comfort him. "You'll find something else, I'm sure. Think of it this way, at least your debut as a lead won't have this hokey dialogue in it."

"I guess." The otter slipped out of the raccoon's grip. "I'm going to go home and see what my agent can dig up." With that, he shuffled for the door, his tail carried low. Max bit his lip and rejoined the other crew. He needed the extra money from doing break down.

՟

It took Max two weeks, but he was able to find an adult production that needed an extra rigger, so he wouldn't have to fluff the actors. In the meantime, he worked a few shifts at the sub shop a friend of his owned for some extra cash. The film Max landed had a higher production value then his last couple of gigs, and the director for this one was pretty serious. He did both porn and standard movies, so he expected a lot out of his crew and films.

Being more excited about this film than anything else he'd been involved with in the last few years, Max gave Carson a call to see how he was doing after the first day of shooting.

"They want me to do another film with Joshua Swanks," Carson said dejectedly over the phone.

"So, that's good, isn't it? That will help build your brand."

"I'm tired of being a two-bit bottom. I mean seriously, it's another one of his gang bang films where he does four to five different guys. I told my agent he needed to find me something better."

"Is there any chance they're going to resume production on 'An Otter on the Serengeti?'"

102

"No," Carson said, exasperated. "Last I heard, they're suing the director. I've got some money in the bank, but I'm tired of not breaking out."

"Would you like to go out for coffee? It would get you out of the house," asked Max. Perhaps that would get the otter's problems off his mind.

Carson paused. "Sure, I can swing that. Tonight at 8?"

"Yeah, how about the place down on Western Ave."

"The Java Box? I've been there."

"Great," said the raccoon. "I'll see you soon."

Max got to the coffee shop early and waited for Carson to show up. He got his drink, then found a comfortable spot in the shop with two big armchairs for them. The otter was late and that had Max worried. It wasn't until he finally showed up that Max could relax back into the chair and stop gripping the arms tightly. Carson first came over to say hellow and then went to order.

When he returned with a hot tea and sat down, he looked tired and fidgety. But he smiled softly at Max after he made himself comfortable.

"Good evening," said Max in his best dramatic voice.

"Hi," said Carson.

"Busy day?" Max asked.

Carson sighed. "Yeah. I've been trying to see if I can find other work. I've been hoping to get something more upmarket, but it's not coming easy."

"I hear ya. I was lucky to land this gig I got right now. The director seems easy to work for, and he doesn't just do adult films. I'm hoping if this goes well, I can get to be a crew member on one of his other movies."

"That would be great," said the otter, sipping his tea.

"I know!" said Max. "We'll see though."

Carson put down his tea and leaned back into the large armchair, letting his body sink into it. The otter sighed again. "I just need to have faith. If nothing comes up soon, I'll do that Joshua Swanks film."

"That will at least get you more exposure."

"I know," said Carson.

"Something better will come around for you."

The otter opened his eyes and glanced at Max when he reached out to pat Carson on his hand.

"I just want to find something real in my life. Something with meaning," said the otter.

"You have me," Max said. The moment he said it, the otter's eyes got a little wide.

"I meant to ask you this, but is this a date?"

Max froze. "A date?"

"Yeah. This is what couples do when they're starting out; they meet up, spend time together alone, and talk."

"Uhh… I dunno," said Max. He hadn't been thinking about it as a date, but that was why he had invited Carson out tonight, hadn't he? He had been thinking a lot about Carson and they weren't always the most wholesome thoughts. Hadn't that been why the otter had invited him out to sushi?

Carson chuckled. "Don't tell me you've forgotten what dating is about."

The raccoon shook his head. "No," he said softly.

"Well then, is it?" asked the otter.

Max sucked in his breath. "I think so. I'm so sorry; I didn't mean to ask you out on a date. I'm…" he blushed.

The otter laughed. "So, this is just an accident?"

"No!" he said. Crap, he didn't want Carson to think he didn't like him. Without pausing, he leaned forward across the armchairs and kissed the otter. It wasn't deep, but it had the promise of something more. Carson shuddered and it wasn't just due to the release of sexual tension.

"Wow," he said. The otter hesitated and then went back for a kiss of his own, deeper and more insistent.

They broke off feeling silly, ears going down as they realized people were staring at them a little.

"Perhaps we should go someplace more private?" said Max.

"Mmm…" said Carson. "That would be nice, but let's save that for later…"

"Then how about I buy us a pastry to split and see where this goes?"

Carson sank back into the chair. "Sure," he said contently. "There is plenty of time for us to explore each other physically another time. It's not like you don't know what I've got." Max got up and started to turn away, but Carson motioned him closer. "But next time you give me a blow job, I'm going to finish."

Max's eyes went big, and his ears went flat against his head. "Well of course, but only if I get to use the ball gag."

Carson frowned. "We'll have to talk about that. I'm not a huge fan."

Max leaned close in and whispered. "Yeah, but you're really hot when you are tied up."

Carson coughed and hid his eyes behind his paws. He looked really embarrassed, but as Max stood up and walked away to get the pastry, he could hear the otter's tail thumping against the chair.

Appearing in Knotted *by Weasel Press back in 2016, this story deals with BDSM and personal health. This is one of my most serious stories, yet also one of my most adult. A warning, one of the characters in this has cancer, and that's a major topic the story deals with.*

A Moment of Darkness

There is a tug on my tail as the last bit of leather securing me is tightened into place. All of the locks are now secure. I feel a tingle of excitement run through my body, knowing what will happen now.

"Are you ready?" my boyfriend asks me, kneeling naked in the bed before me. Ezra is smiling, his bushy coyote tall wagging behind him. His expressive ears are perked forward, waiting for my response. I know he wants to put on a good show for me.

I nod softly. "Yes, sir."

"Is the big wolf scared what the lanky coyote will do to him?" His voice is musical, and it's a rhetorical question. I wouldn't be going through with this if I didn't trust him.

I pull at my wrists, feeling the resistance. They are held together in soft leather handcuffs. A cord runs from them across the bed down to where the rope is tied to the frame. The feeling of being secured is familiar. For a moment, I'm reminded of the tape and gauze used to secure an IV drip to my arm, but the positioning is different. I shake my head to push that association away.

"Ammar, are you sure you are ready?" he asks me again, this time in his normal tone. He must have noticed the expression on my face. "I'm doing this for you."

I breathe in, feeling the leather of the harness I wear stretch against my fur. Today is the first day I've been strong enough for this in a while. He wanted me to rest today, but I haven't felt this good in weeks. I don't know when I'll feel this good again. "I know. I'm ready, Ezra."

"Okay," he says, pulling out a piece of black cloth. "Close your eyes."

Obediently, I do. I can feel the cloth being wrapped around my head and the brush of Ezra's paws as they touch my ears. Then there is the jerking motion as Ezra ties the blindfold behind my head.

"Is that good?" he asks. "I made sure the fabric is thick enough."

I open my eyes. I can only see shadows now. "Yeah," I whisper.

"Okay." The rope connects the cuffs on my forepaws to the spreader bar attached to the cuffs on my hindpaws, and I feel it shift as he moves around on the bed. My nose tickles with a familiar scent, and I feel a brush of fur against my muzzle, and then there is the scent of his maleness. There is more movement, though, and the ropes and my elbows dip as the bed shifts.

"Does the wolfie know what he wants?" comes Ezra's voice teasingly to my ears.

I whimper, putting need into my voice.

"Now I can't have you whimpering like that." he says. He shifts on the bed, the mattress creaking, and I come face to face with his cock when he baps me with it and rubs the tip against my lips.

I dart my tongue out, getting the taste into my muzzle before I take him into my mouth. The smell is intense and floods my diminished senses. Through the blindfold, I can't see what he's doing, but I hear the distinct clink of metal.

He pulls himself away from me, taking the treat from my wet muzzle. "Oh no. You've been bad. You don't deserve that. You know what that means?" The question hangs there.

I lower my ears. "Yes, sir." I can already smell the rubber of the gag. Scent is also why I know I will have a chance. My natural scent had begun to change, and Ezra picked up on that. My natural musk had started to take on a sour smell. It's what prompted me to make the first doctor's appointment.

"Open wide, and I promise not to leave you like this."

I inhale sharply. That is against the rules of the session. Ezra said he wasn't sure he wanted to do this, but I'd insisted. I wanted to let him know I trusted him unlike anyone I've ever been with before, that our bond is stronger than any I've had before. My feet are bound, my hands are bound, and the rope running across the bed means I can't move either of those more than a few inches. I am completely at his mercy. That's why he can't leave me like this.

"Is that talk too dirty? Your ears just went all the way back," he asks me.

"I… no. But we talked about that."

I feel his hand scratching between my ears, trying to re-assure me. "Relax. I promise I won't do anything to you you didn't ask for. Do you want to proceed now? Once I put the gag on, anything I ask you will be a yes or no question."

"Go ahead," I say.

"Okay," the coyote says. "Open up."

I open my muzzle wide, and I feel the taste of rubber as the ball gag is slipped into my muzzle. I can feel Ezra's paws at the back of my head as he fastens the gag and then checks to make sure it's secure. He shifts, the ropes stretching. It feels like he's reaching for something, because a few seconds later, I feel him move again. Something is pressed into my left hand.

"That's the clicker. At any point, if you need me to stop, use it. Click once to get me to continue what I'm doing or to say yes. Click it twice to say no or to stop because it's uncomfortable. Three or more times, and I'm ending the scene entirely. Now, do you understand?"

This is how I know we can do this safely. It's what we decided to use as a replacement for a safe word since I can't talk around the gag in my muzzle. I already know he's going to make me whimper for him to stop, but I instructed him to keep going until I use the clicker. I need to do this. I have to be strong for Ezra, but I can't be all the time. In this brief respite between the cycles of treatment I am going to have to go through, I need to let my guard down.

I squeeze the clicker once to let him know I have it.

"Then you are my piece of tail now, Ammar. You're mine until I see fit to release you from your bindings, you filthy wolf!" He laughs, keeping the lilt in his voice. "Or you stop it." This, he delivers in his normal tone. "Now, where was I?"

The scent of male coyote, rubber, and leather is strong in my nose. I feel Ezra's hand on my head, guiding me. Then I feel the heat as he rubs his cock on top of my muzzle and I'm forced to sniff at his balls. Instinctually, I want to dart my tongue out at them, to take them into my muzzle, but I can't. The gag keeps my mouth frozen open.

"Is this what you want?" he asks, rubbing his cock along my muzzle. I'm not sure exactly how hard he is, but he already feels aroused. His scent has taken on that predatory, sexy musk I'm used to experiencing when we have sex. My own erection bobs under me, the anticipation of the moment as we worked to set up the scene has left me aching for a while. I'm waiting for him to sate the lust inside of me.

I whimper, but Ezra's hand pushes me against his stiff member. "Don't act like you don't want this."

Oh god, do I want this. The scent alone is driving me crazy. I pull at the bindings holding me. My tail is held in place by a cuff that connects with the collar I'm wearing, so it curls. It's not easy to get a wolf's tail to curl, but mine is curled right now, just like a husky's. We both know what I want; he's just delaying the inevitable.

But that's life, isn't it? The inevitable is always around the corner. I push that thought out of my mind. I don't want to think about that right now. I know where that leads: back to the doctors and the IV. I don't have to return there for another week. I don't have to be strong again until then. For the moment, I can be weak, and Ezra is all that matters.

He pushes my head down so he can rub the bottom of his cock against my wet nose. I feel him shiver at the touch and my breath before he pulls away and the bed creaks loudly. The ropes holding me pull taut and relax, and then there is nothing. No sensation, and no sound but my own muffled breathing and the sound of the blood in my ears.

My ears naturally flick back and forth, trying to locate where the coyote went. I think he's standing in front of the bed, but the rush of blood in my head and in my cock is making it hard for me to focus.

I try to move, and while I can shift around a little, the metal locks on my cuffs jingle and pull. If I click the clicker once to tell him to continue, will that bring him back? If I click it once, will he continue doing whatever he is doing now?

I whine in frustration, my ears back. I don't want him to stop. A soft chuckle comes from in front of me. "You don't want to wait, do you?" he asks.

I click the clicker twice.

"Okay, okay, but I'm admiring the view. That tail looks amazing."

I whine again, ears still back, and I can hear the click of his claws on the floor. Suddenly, there is a slap on my ass, and I yelp, but it comes out muffled around the gag. I nearly choke on the ball in my mouth.

He chuckles. I feel my weight shift as the bed creaks, and then a paw traces down my stomach toward my groin, stopping to flick at the tip of my cock. The brush of his fur against my legs and the feeling of my knees sinking down into the mattress tells me he has gotten on the bed behind me.

"Someone is excited, I see." he whispers, as he flicks my cock again, letting it bob in the air.

Damn you, Ezra. Why must you tease me? I know the answer is because I want him to tease me, to take his time. I'm the one who devised the rope setup. I'm the one who ordered the leather cuffs and had them sized to my wrists. I'm the one who told him what to do, and I'm the one whose cock is throbbing in the air as the coyote bats at it playfully. I know when he finally gives me my release, it will be sweeter than any dessert I could ever put into my muzzle.

I growl a little as he bats at my stiffness again. The muffled noise barely registers as a growl in my own ears.

"The overgrown puppy doesn't like that?" I feel a paw slide up toward my hip. It's a question, and I think for a moment before I click the clicker twice.

He huffs, and for a moment, there's nothing, just his hand resting on my hip.

"Too bad," he says, reaching down to flick my cock again.

I growl as loud as I can with a ball gag in my throat. It would be menacing if it didn't have the ball in my mouth. Instead, it sounds a bit like someone is being strangled.

"Okay, okay. I get it," says the coyote, exasperated at me. "You said you wanted to be teased."

I did. I told him he could tease me, but that doesn't mean I like it. I pull at the cuffs, but they hold my place. I had him put a spreader bar between my ankles so I wouldn't fall over, so I don't have much range of motion back there. Suddenly, I freeze when I feel it.

His hand is still resting on my hip, but now a finger is tracing the opening of my ass gently, poking at me.

"This is what you want, Ammar, isn't it?" he sinks a digit into me, exploring. It sends a shiver up my spine as he probes me. "Something hard buried deep inside you?"

I whine loudly, needy. Even with the gag in place, the desire is obvious.

"That's not a yes," he laughs, his voice musical sounding.

Bastard coyote! My form of canine is almost the same as his. Us wolves use the same expressions as coyotes. He can read the tension in my restrained body like an open book. I click the clicker once.

He laughs and sinks a second finger into my quivering rear. "I thought so."

I just stay where I am, knees and elbows bent on the slick vinyl sheets we put on our king-sized bed. The sheets are something Ezra came up with. There is nothing I can do except wait to see what he does.

His paw that isn't probing me slips down to grasp my shaft as he shifts his weight and presses his cock up against the side of my rump. The heat and slight slickness of my drool still on the shaft drags through my fur. The coyote's tail is probably wagging, but I can't tell. My blood is pounding in my ears now. It sounds like a freight train in my head.

Slowly, he pulls out and the paw on my cock leaves. I feel him shift, and he fumbles with something. There's a distinct pop, and then I squirm as cool lube is poured directly on my ass, letting it run down the cleft. His paw returns to probe at my insides, slickening them up.

My ears are back, and my whines come freely, headily. I need this. I really need this. I can't see what he's doing to me, but I can feel it. I'm having to get used to not being able to see things that are important in my life. This is just practice for what I'm going through.

When Ezra pulls his fingers out, I can hear the sound of him slickening up his shaft, before the bed creaks and something hard slides up the cleft of my butt to rest between my ass cheeks.

He doesn't say anything, and the way I whine leaves no doubt what I want. He takes a minute to rub himself up and down before he pulls back. He lines up and starts to press himself in, mounting me. I feel my body tense, and then it relaxes. This is it. He's done teasing me, I think. We're at the meat and potatoes of tonight's play session now. All the gear, all the trust I put in him, this is it. We're really doing this. I open my hands to brace myself by pushing my shoulders up as much as I can, letting the tension flow out of me as the fucking I've longed for begins. I drop the clicker onto the bed.

I freeze, and as I feel the last inch of Ezra's cock sink into me it hits me, then; I've lost control of the scene. As far as the coyote knows, if he thrusts too rough or gets creative in a way that hurts, I'll signal for him to stop, but I just lost that ability. A deep panic sets into me, then, the coyote slowly teasing my ass with his cock, oblivious to my panic. I need the clicker so he can't hurt me. I need that, that little bit of control.

A paw slaps my rump as he grips at my tail base, starting to thrust. "You like this?" he asks me.

I whine, panicking as I try to find the clicker, patting the sheets with my paws. Where is it?

Ezra misreads my motions. Maybe his eyes are closed, savoring the moment, but he wuffs happily. "You are so tight, hun. You haven't been this excited in a long time. I'm glad to see you're into it."

Crap, I'm already clenching down on him, and that's starting to hurt. If I could just look with my eyes, I could find the clicker, but I'm still blindfolded. *Damn it!* I set up the rules for this. I said we should use the gag. I suggested the blindfold. And now, now I'm slapping the mattress looking for the signal device I bought.

I push myself up on the pads of my paws, and I feel something by my right hand. I seize it and grasp the clicker, as Ezra thrusts himself into me. I squeeze it so tight, it clicks once.

Ezra freezes. "Is everything alright? Did I push you too hard?" he asks. The hand at my tail base slips down to my hips. He's about to pull out; I can tell. Frantically, I click it again. I don't want him to stop.

"You sure?" he asks, his voice no longer containing any playfulness in it.

I managed to get out a 'mmph' around the gag and click again. Ezra pulls back, but then buries it into me deep. I squeeze my eyes shut even though the blindfold is covering them.

He begins to slam himself into me roughly, all measures of decorum lost now. He pushes me forward on the bed with his thrusts, but I can't move, and all I can do is push back as I strain against my bonds. He buries himself repeatedly to the hilt inside of me, each thrust accompanied with a loud coyote grunt.

The feeling of being filled by Ezra is amazing. I can feel his knot popping in and out of me as it swells. My tongue wants to roll out of my muzzle in a blissful pant, but I can't because of the gag. My tail wants to wag, but it's still stuck in that forced curl. All I can do is fight against my bindings. They keep me snug, but that's the point: it's not moving I want to do, I want to feel the tension due to the fact I can't move. I want to test my strength against the tight leather and feel it holding me back.

The creaking of the bed is loud in my ears, so it catches me by surprise when Ezra pushes himself forward and lets himself fall forward, settling his weight directly on top of me. In the process, he pins my already abused tail against my back. I want to touch myself so badly now, driving myself to my finish, but all I can do it wait until Ezra does the work for me. My cock throbs, wanting its release.

"Who's my wolf?" he whispers into my left ear, nibbling at it. I whine in response, my submission to him complete. In this moment, I'm just his. I've forgotten about everything else, even the cancer inside of me that is slowly killing me. It's blissful as I squirm and moan at the touch. A free hand finds one of my nipples, gently tracing a claw over it before he wraps a paw around my aching member.

"Have you been naughty enough for me to let you have your release, or should I leave you cuffed liked this?"

I thrust myself into his paw as best as I can with my limited mobility as he grinds his knot against my ass.

"I'm not hearing the clicker, love."

Damn you, Ezra! I click it once.

"That's a good wolf," he coos into my ear, nibbling at the tip. I feel him pop the knot in before he pulls it out again. The paw gently traces my shaft as he repeats the motion. His touch is light, his thrusts hard, and it drives me crazy. I screw my eyes shut, panting around the gag, trying to suck down more oxygen. He keeps doing this motion of popping the knot in and out of my abused body, pushing me up toward the edge until it's too much.

I don't feel the first steps of my own climax; the feelings are just too intense. I'm just aware of Ezra gripping me tightly. I paint the slick vinyl sheets with my seed, my body shivering, Ezra's knot grinding up in me. The tension against my bonds drives me crazy. It's been too long since we've had a session this intense. Even spent with his weight on top of me, I can't let myself down. I have to hold this position with my exhausted body.

I'm clenching too hard, and his knot is too swollen for me to release him, so he nips at the scruff of my neck as he proceeds to work the shaft stuck within me now. I feel the grunting coyote tense and then the telltale yip he makes when he cums.

Between panting around the scruff of my neck, I can hear his voice. "Oh god yes, Ammar… I should fuck you like this all the time." I wouldn't mind that, so I click the clicker again, and he attempts to laugh with a muzzle full of wolf fur. "We'll have to see if there is time to do something so involved next time." He licks affectionately at my neck. I'm not due for another chemotherapy session until next week, so hopefully I can feel his warmth and love like this again soon.

I wag my pinned tail as best as I can. We're tied now. My breathing is still ragged; the gag isn't making it easy for me to catch my breath. I can feel his body pulsing like a storm in my ears. In this moment, there is just him, and with his body wrapped around me, I feel safe. My submission to him may be complete, but his protection and love of me is even more powerful. I don't have to be strong right now, and that's a relief. He can be strong for the both of us in this moment.

I feel a hand at the back of my head, and the click and tug of metal and leather as the buckle for the gag is undone. Once I feel the straps loosen, I shake and let it fall out of my mouth, where the wet slippery rubber bounces against my paws. I work my jaw to get some feeling back into it. The blindfold is pulled back, and I'm forced to blink at the sudden influx of light.

"How are you feeling?" Ezra asks me.

"Filled," I say, wiggling my tied rump. My voice is sandpapery from using the ball gag.

"Beyond that, this is the most restrained you've ever been during sex. You didn't have any nausea, did you?"

"No, the medication is keeping that under control. I'm sore but satisfied." I close my eyes. "I know you're there for me, protecting me." And it's not just that; there's something else. "I know I can trust you."

The coyote chuckles. "Silly wolf, you've always been able to trust me. Five years, and you're just starting to think that way?"

I pull at my restraints, still fully in place. "It's not just that. It's a deeper type of trust." I still have him locked inside of me, but he's already softened. He could pull out already, I'm sure. He's holding the connection for me. "I don't need to worry. I know when I need you to, you'll be there for me. I can let down my barriers with you, and I can let you in, in a way I can't do with other people. I can also let myself be weak in these moments."

"This sounds like that pack stuff you wolves love so much."

I shift my weight, fighting him and my bonds. "Isn't exposing yourself, your throat, and your body to someone you love like this, and knowing they're there for you, isn't that beyond simple pack bonds? Isn't it a trust exercise in our commitment to each other?"

The coyote whispers into my ear as he breathes on it and nips at the tip very gently. "Oh, it is, but I need you to be strong for me."

I'm doing the best I can for him. We're lucky we caught the pancreatic cancer so early, thanks to Ezra's nose. I never would have noticed the change in my scent myself. Even better, the cancer is only in Stage I, and for this type, the doctors tell me the five year survival rate is over eighty percent.

"I am doing everything I can," I whisper. "Like I have to trust you'll let me off the bed, you have to trust me. I'm fighting."

The coyote laughs and nips lovingly at the back of my neck, pressing his weight down on top of me. "I know, Ammar. I try not to think of what might happen. It doesn't make things better."

No, it doesn't. I've already run over the scenarios in my mind. I'm not there in all of them.

"Ezra, I wanted to ask you something?"

"Yes, my love?"

"Do you want to get married, Ezra? We've been dating long enough. I realize we may not have much time left together, but it feels like the right thing."

He doesn't say anything, He's silent for a minute before he slips out of me. There's a pop, and I can feel the release of his pent-up fluids from inside of me. "I'm not sure now is the right time to propose." The bed creaks as he moves around on it, taking his weight off of me.

"Sorry, I just feel vulnerable." I've felt vulnerable for a while now. There are varying levels of vulnerability that I'm learning to deal with.

He moves forward on the bed so he can look at me. A hand strokes my back, and I turn to see him looking at me. "We said we were going to wait."

I sigh. "Yeah, well things have changed."

"I'm willing to do it, but are you sure now is a good time? I mean, you're still tied up and all messy."

Even though he is a loving mate, he's still a coyote. "Not now! You know what I mean."

He smirks. "I figured you wanted to wait until you felt better."

He knows as well as I do that it's not guaranteed I'll beat this into remission. Even then, it could come back later.

"I don't want to be alone." Isn't that the point of what we just did? I need to feel I belong in his life, that with the diagnosis and treatment that he's there, and I still belong to him.

"Ammar, a ring isn't going to make me hold you any tighter. These straps aren't going to make me love you more. I'm already giving you my all." His ears are back, his yellow eyes piercing.

There is the strength I need when I can't summon more of my own to keep fighting. Knowing I can keep being with such a loving mate is the resolve I need to make it to all those appointments during the chemotherapy cycle. I want to cry with how beautiful he makes me feel. He doesn't see the disease living inside of me when he looks at me.

"I want to because I know no one else will ever be there for me like you." I really want to wrap myself around him right now, but I can't. I'm still cuffed to the bed. "And can you help me out of all this gear? It makes it hard for me to give you the hug you deserve for sticking with me through this."

He chuckles and reaches for the key on the nightstand. "How about after the next treatment cycle, we go to the justice of the peace and make it official instead of breaking out all the gear?"

My heart soars. I'm going to be part of the eighty percent. I'm going to beat this. With Ezra's loving embrace, I am strong enough to get through this. "How about both?" I suggest as he starts to unlock my wrists.

He shakes his head. "You, sir, have a one-track mind."

"With a beautiful mate like you, why shouldn't I indulge when I can?"

The coyote blushes, and I feel warmth spreading through my body. Fuck cancer. I'm not going to let it take this away from me.

Published in BREEDS: Wolves *by Thurston Howl Publications in 2018, Unsatisfied is set a few months after* A Moment of Darkness *and continues the story, this time exploring chastity and patience.*

Unsatisfied

I whine. I whine like I need it more than life itself, even though I know that is a lie. I need my life more than anything else, but right now I would like to forget that fact. I want to feel something other than my current predicament. The cage grasping my manhood is itching, and it has been itching all week. I need it to come off.

"Hush wolf. I already know what you want, and I can't do that. You told me when it could come off," Ezra remarks, looking up from the book he is reading. I got it for him a month ago, as a wedding gift. Tonight is one of the few times he's been able to sit down and read it.

I pull at the soft leather cuffs that have me tied to the footboard of the bed. "We agreed, it would be tonight," I plead. I haven't been able to get my hands on my shaft except in the mornings when he lets me shower without the cage. We bathe together so there can be no cheating.

The coyote glances at the clock by the bedside. I know it reads ten minutes after six without looking myself. I've been watching the clock, counting the minutes as they go by. "We agreed on 8 PM," Ezra says.

"Why are you being such a stickler for the time?"

Ezra sighs and puts the book down. "Because you are tiring me out, Ammar."

I grumble and pull against the straps that keep me kneeling on the ground. My tail wags, although most of it is under the bed. "Me, tire you out? Isn't it the other way around?" I tilt my head just a little trying to portray an innocence he knows I don't have.

He smirks at me, showing me some fang. "I assure you, it's all you."

I huff. "We're not getting any younger. I'll tell you where I put my key if you let me free."

Ezra chuckles and kicks back in the chair. The coyote is naked except for the leather harness he wears. He spreads his legs, showing me his own caged maleness. "One of us can wait."

I do a lot of waiting nowadays: waiting for the doctor, waiting for test results, waiting for the nausea that comes after chemo to pass. Now I'm waiting for when he deems me worthy of having another orgasm.

I growl low at him. "You just like teasing me."

He gets up and walks over to me so I have to look up at him. He looms over me, grinning, the black harness standing out against his tan and cream fur. "You love every minute of it," he whispers to me, tracing his hand along the side of my muzzle into my cheek fluff.

My ears fall back, and I whine again. "Please, Ezra."

"We said eight o'clock. You are the one who gave us this challenge."

"And you are cheating." He's the one who suggested I get ready and strap up and get in position. He knows being in this position causes me to get hard. I thought he wanted to start early. I didn't realize he planned to leave me in this position for over two hours. I'm aching for him to free me now. Everything we do currently is timed around my treatment sessions with their carefully administered IV drips. It would be nice for once if we could be free of regimented routines for a while. I thought this would be one of those spontaneous moments.

He smiles and curls his tongue around his fangs. "Did I ever say coyotes play fair?"

I reach out and nip at the caged cock, trying to catch the metal in my mouth. Immediately I feel a finger digging in under my lips. "No! Drop it."

I let go and sigh. "Fine."

"You are going to catch my shaft with a fang if you do that," he says, checking over his maleness through the cage.

"I didn't mean to," I reply.

"Oh, yeah, you got me right here," he says with a wince, poking at a spot of fur on his sheath. "I think I need to take this off and clean it."

"If you let me up I can get the key," I offer.

He shakes his head. "Just tell me where the key is."

I give Ezra a look. "No..."

"It hurts, Ammar," he pleads.

Crap, the last thing I want to do is hurt him. "It's over on my key ring on top of the dresser."

He walks over to the dresser and picks up my keys. It takes him a minute, but he gets the chastity device off, which he leaves on the dresser with my keys.

"Oh god, this is a relief," he says, walking back over to me playing with himself.

"You bastard!" I yell, realizing he used this as an excuse to get me to let his shaft go free.

"It was starting to really ache." He gently strokes himself, his erection growing.

"This isn't fair!" I protest, ears falling back.

"Is it?" he asks, gently bringing his crotch up to my muzzle. "I told you. Coyotes don't play fair."

"Spork."

He freezes when I use our safe word, big triangle ears pointing straight up "That's it?"

"This isn't what we agreed to."

"Ammar…"

"Spork!"

He flattens his ears. "Sorry. I thought you would like this. I was going to get the dildo out and let you ride it next."

It's always tempting to have something up there. Those are some of the most blissful moments of my life. I don't think during those times. I don't worry about my uncertain future. I'm just me.

The doctor told me yesterday I'm in partial remission. That just means I have more waiting to do. Maybe the cancer will get worse, maybe it won't. Maybe this is the best the treatment program can give me, and I'll be part of the twenty percent who don't survive for five years or more. I don't know. I take each day as they come.

But I know one thing: I need to get this shit off my mind.

I look up at his concerned expression. "And then you'll let me out of the cage?"

He nods. "After you've been good and teased, I'll let you go. I'll let you lie back and I will jerk you off."

I smile as innocent as I can, knowing what he plans for me. It sounds nice, and my pent-up frustration will be released. "Okay, you can continue."

He chuckles, gently running his paw across my cheek to scratch at my right ear. "You sure now?"

I nod.

Ezra turns around, letting his tail get up in my face. "Now, where is that dildo you like?"

Since I'm under his tail, I take this opportunity to bury my snout against his ass cheeks. The musk under there is strong, but I plant my cold nose right into his cleft and lick.

"Hey now!" says Ezra, surprised, pulling away before I can do more to him.

I give him my best innocent look, one ear cocked up while the other is down. My tail thumps against the ground. This provokes a chuckle.

"Right…" he says, "like I would ever believe that face." He goes to our vertical dresser and fishes a dildo out of the toy drawer along with a bottle of lube. Tonight he pulls out the black canine toy with its sizeable knot. It's filling, but not so big I can't handle it. He comes back smirking. The coyote proceeds to slick it up with lube. Then after kneeling down next to me, he squirts more lube onto his hand.

"Up," he commands, patting on my rump and I push myself up. First he sticks a slickened finger in, quickly lubing me up before he places the dildo on top of the towel under me. I can feel the tip of the toy against my ass. "Okay, slowly now," he says, still holding the toy for me.

Carefully, I lower myself. At first the toy slips out, but with Ezra's guidance, I can feel the tip and head of the canine toy sink into me. Once it's in securely, Ezra wipes his paw on the towel and gets up to stand before me.

"Come on now," he coos to me, "show me what a good wolf you are," he adds, letting his semi hard member hang in front of me.

I love the scent of my coyote. His musk always excites me with its rich, earthy qualities. It makes me think of both the intimate moments we have together and the feeling of safety I have with Ezra. I lean forward and gently take him into my muzzle. Ezra stiffens quickly at my touch, and my restrained shaft also tries to harden. The pent-up frustration between my legs gets worse, and I have trouble ignoring the grasp of metal against my sheath.

Ezra lets me suck on him for a minute before he steps forward, forcing me to pull back a little and relax my leg muscles. The toy worms itself deeper inside of me. The pressure in my groin is becoming unbearable. I desperately want to touch myself, or have Ezra touch me. Instead, I'm working the coyote's shaft with quick bobbing motions while he scratches behind my ears. This is worse than when he normally handcuffs me so I can't handle my cock. With the chastity device, I can't even express how horny I am right now.

Oh god. Oh god. I need to get out of this cage. The metal around my shaft is tight. The pressure against it blunts everything else. The smell and taste of Ezra alone is enough to drive me crazy, but the pressure under my tail makes it worse. I can't really bob on the toy in this position, but the little motion I can do is agonizing. My cock desperately wants to get hard, but it can't.

It is in this moment of need that I can feel the numbness starting. It's not the urges of my desire becoming just a blinding white noise in my mind, but the exhaustion that comes on suddenly sometimes after chemotherapy. I can feel the weakness in my arms and legs start. While it's been two weeks since my last chemo session, I feel all my energy starting to sap away. In this moment of intense pleasure my body is reminding me I'm still sick.

Even though I try and fight it, I can feel my legs go and the toy's knot sinks straight into me as I drop all my weight down on the dildo. I gasp around Ezra's cock from the knot's sudden intrusion deep inside of me.

Ezra takes a half-step back, trying to gauge my reaction, but I follow him. I'm not going to let this keep me from finishing him off. I can do this. I want to make him happy and while I can feel my arms starting to tremble, I can finish this. I don't want to leave him disappointed.

If the coyote realizes I'm starting to struggle, he'll stop, but he's close right now. He knows if I can't continue I'll give him a sign, or use our safe word. I give my tail a wag and he keeps going, thrusting into my muzzle. I can do this. Cancer is not going to take this away from me. He is my yote, and I am his wolf. We have mutual needs to satisfy, and until he climaxes, I won't feel like I've done my part right.

I press on, and Ezra murmurs happily. The pleasure is gone, but he doesn't know that. He thrusts into my muzzle hard a few more times before he pulls back and out. He splatters his seed across my face and paints my chest. A few drops land on my tongue as it rolls out.

I fall back panting. I got him off, but my arms are visibly shaking now.

Ears tilt and as he looks at me. "Ammar?" he asks me questioningly.

"Spork," I pant out.

"Fuck," he says, dropping to his knees. He quickly unclips one cuff, and then reaches for the other while supporting my weight. He presses himself against me, and I can feel the bite of his harness against my sticky fur. I'm panting from exhaustion and vertigo when I lower my arms. My whole body is shaking.

"Are you okay?" Ezra asks me, kneeling next to me, holding onto me. "I didn't realize this would be so taxing on you."

"I'll be okay. My muscles gave out on me for a minute."

"Can you get up on your knees?" Ezra asks me. "Let me get the toy out."

I nod and with his help, he pulls me up and gently tugs out the dildo. He drops it with a plop onto the floor. Carefully he helps me lie down, and I accidently kick the toy under the bed.

"Rest for a minute, while I get the key."

I nod and just pant while he gets the key and frees me from the cage. It's a relief and even though my body is exhausted, I can feel my cock harden a little while Ezra checks to make sure I'm okay. Gently he strokes along my side, tan fingers playing through gray fur. I'm able to give him a little wag to let him know I'll be fine.

"I think I wore out my wolfie," he says.

"Not complaining."

"Yeah, but I still haven't gotten you off. I don't want you to feel unsatisfied."

I chuckle, lying on the ground. My limbs are numb. "It will be okay. Tomorrow?"

He whines. "I didn't want to make this about just me."

I close my eyes. "It will be fine. I'm still fighting for us."

I know he's worried, but he keeps up a brave face. He tells me things will be okay now even when I know they won't be. I hate that he's adapted to the stress of dealing with my illness that way, but with his help I keep fighting. I keep hoping there is a life for us together on the other side of this. As long as I don't give up, I'll make it there.

I look up into his amber eyes. I can see him wanting to say something or do something that will push me on, and bring me to that climax my body has denied me from having. He knows though from experience he can't, and I hate that he can't.

After he lets me lie there for a few minutes, the coyote carefully helps me stand up and then guides me into a comfortable position on top of the bed with its vinyl sheets. I leave a sticky stain on them from the lube and cum. I'm grateful in this moment I don't have to worry about the bed. We put these on today because we weren't sure what we wanted to do. I have a lot of good memories about me and Ezra on this bed. Normally after a play session we change the bed back to our regular cotton sheets, but I'm too spent. My muscles are still twitching from the exhaustion.

He gets up and comes back with a towel to sponge out the cum from my fur and wipe lube off my rump. When he's done cleaning me up, he drapes a blanket over me.

"Do you want me to call your doctor?" he asks me, worry across his face.

I shake my head. "I'm just tired. It will pass."

He nods and leaves me for a minute, and I just lie there, trying to still my racing heart. Finally, Ezra comes back and gets on the bed. He's still wearing the harness. He wraps his arms around me, and I feel him press a small metal key into my right paw. I can feel something hard and metallic pressed against my rump.

He whispers into my ear, "When you're ready, we'll continue this."

I smile to myself and finger the key to his chastity device. "I love you, Ezra," I whisper back finally.

The coyote squeezes his arms tight around me. "I know and I love you too, Ammar. I'm here for you. I know you can beat this."

My tail wags between us. I'm not sure I can beat cancer, but it is the moments like this where I know I need to keep fighting. Safe and protected, I doze off with his tan arms wrapped around my grey-furred body.

Set in 1950s Las Vegas, The Road to Midnight *originally appeared back in 2016 in* FANG Volume 7, *published by FurPlanet. This is the same volume that contains Splatters. Against the backdrop of atomic age America, two souls share a night that shows them who they are and how small we all are when faced with the relentless march of progress.*

The Road to Midnight

The lobby of the Desert Sun Hotel and Casino is brightly lit, with earth toned walls and furniture. My natural dusty colored fur with tan and black highlights fits well. The ad that brought me here didn't say they wanted a swift fox, but I think my fur's coloration helped seal the deal. As head concierge, I cut a striking path through the lobby in my dark suits whenever I'm summoned to solve guest issues. Staffing issues, like the one just brought to my attention, don't require such a striking look. For those, I have to listen carefully and make the right call for the hotel.

The raccoon in front of me is smartly dressed, like all our croupiers. Her ringed tail is still and calm, but I can see annoyance on her face. "We've been counting. He's gone through most of his week's wages already," she says to me.

The he Joanna is talking about is our lounge singer. The coyote is a big name in New York, and while he's only been here for two months, he's proving to be a bigger problem than I'd like.

"Mr. Lopez is free to spend his money however he wants."

"I know, but I thought you might want to make sure he could pay his tab and room. He respects you."

I smile at her with practiced ease even though I wish she hadn't brought this issue to my attention. "His room comes complementary. It's in his contract."

She wrings her hands. "Yeah, but you two are, you know, similar."

I let the smile fade. I have more discretion than the coyote about my own affairs. I know all about Mr. Lopez's dalliances back in New York just from reading the papers. He's got a great voice and an excellent repertoire of popular love songs, but he's only here because he's trying to rebuild his reputation. So far he is not doing a good job at that.

"I have guests coming in still, Joanna. They've been coming in all day to see tomorrow's test. Perhaps the GM—"

"He went home already," she says, interrupting me, and puts her hand on my shoulder. "Come on, Antwon. From one fairy to another, you can talk some sense into him."

I cough and straighten myself up. "And Mr. Lopez's 'girlfriend'?"

"I think she may try to kill him if he keeps at it."

I sigh and check my watch. I still have an hour before I can go home. Someone needs to step in before we have another incident. "All right, where is he?"

The coyote is trashed. His motions have become uncoordinated, and the way he is carrying himself makes it obvious. I would have thought there was a limit to how much whisky someone could consume, but for this coyote, that didn't seem to matter. He's ordered enough drinks to collect a small army of them on the poker table. I hang back for a minute to observe before I step in. Joanna leaves me to intervene alone as she goes back to her table to start a new game.

The woman on his arm doesn't appear pleased about being with him. She's supposed to be dating him, but if you've watched them around the hotel enough, you know it's a cover story. A black coyote, she is an aspiring Hollywood actress. She's here because it's helping her career. I still can't decide if her pelt is natural or a dye job, but if it's a dye job, it's the best I've ever seen.

"Well." He leers across the table at a mountain lion betting against him. "Are you going to fold or not?"

He's got some bravado going, considering the mountain lion is slowly cleaning him out. He may be too drunk to realize it's liquid courage at this point. Obviously, the mountain lion has noticed it is.

"Why? You afraid I might leave before you can win your money back?"

Mr. Lopez snorts and pushes another chip into the pot. "Let's make this interesting."

The lion quirks an ear and tosses another chip out. "Call."

"Two Pair."

"Three of a kind."

The coyote sags back. "Shit." As the mountain lion stacks the chips, it does look like Mr. Lopez has lost his entire week's wages.

"I told you, you should have stopped drinking," his girl says.

"Oh, you told me, huh?" He turns to her. "Maybe there is a reason I'm drinking, toots."

She huffs and gets up. "You are an awful man, Jacob."

"Well, how about that, I'm now a broke, awful man!"

She shakes her head and walks off. He sits back in his chair looking at his depleted stack of chips.

"You want another round?" he asks the mountain lion.

"You might want to quit while you still have something, Mr. Lopez," I suggest, stepping in.

He glances over at me. "Antwon?" He smiles. "Oh good, we need some fresh blood at this table. Dealer, deal him in. I need to win at least a few drinks back. I can't have this guy walking off with all my money."

The dealer, a red fox, glances up at me, but I shake my head. "I can't gamble on the clock, Mr. Lopez. If you don't mind, I think it's time to get you back to your room."

He sighs and starts collecting his chips. "It's only 10:30 you know, Antwon. The night is still young."

It really doesn't bother me if Mr. Lopez blows all his money in our casino, but it's my job as the head concierge to make sure the entertainment for our hotel isn't drunk under a table. I've been considering asking the bartenders to water down Jacob's drinks. It probably wouldn't help.

Finally, I get Jacob up and moving. He insists on cashing out his remaining chips. The cashier hands him back forty-three dollars of the two hundred he probably started the night with. He proceeds to try and slip me a five as I guide him back to his room.

"You know, you don't have to tip me, sir."

He laughs. "Just take the money. When a man such as me reaches a point like this, it's important to make sure the people in your life know that you appreciate them."

I don't know what that means. I only met Mr. Lopez two months ago when we hired him to be our lounge singer. So far he's been good for business when he's not causing trouble. He's occupied one of the few suites at the casino since then. Since he seems to have a gambling problem, it's a good perk for him.

We turn off the casino floor and reach the part of the hotel where our premier guests stay. I bring Mr. Lopez to his room at the end of the short corridor and wait while he fishes out his key. I'm thankful he finds it and didn't lose it this time.

He sticks the key in the lock. "Did you want to come in, Antwon? I can order you a drink on room service."

I cough, and make sure to keep my tail in a neutral position to hide my annoyance. "I'm still on the clock, Mr. Lopez."

"You are always on the clock when I see you," he remarks, turning to me, having to brace himself against the doorframe of the half-opened entry. "Why is that?"

I blink. "I work here, just like you."

He wags and grins at me. "Yeah, but all I do is sing. You, you keep this place moving and everything clean and organized. Don't you deserve a night off?"

Maybe the alcohol is having more effect on him than I expected. "I do have days off, sir. I'm also not a world-renowned singer from New York City."

"Ah, New York. I miss her you know. But you, you deserve a night off."

I chuckle and wag my tail. "I'm off on Mondays and Tuesdays, so I won't see you till this Wednesday."

"Oh good! Give me a call in the morning, Antwon. It will be good to see you when you're off the clock. You're always so formal on the clock. You, uh, know the number, right?"

"Yes, Mr. Lopez, but—"

"Excellent!" he pushes himself off the door frame and teeters. I reach forward to grab him, and I help him into the room. I can at least feel myself relax after I get the door closed. There will be no one in here besides me to listen to whatever silly thing he says next.

Mr. Lopez has a honeymoon suite to himself. The room is larger than our other rooms. A large bed fills up the center of the room, along with a desk and a small sitting area on one side. Tossed onto the floor in the sitting area is a morning newspaper, along with a glass and a bottle of scotch on the end table. It looks like he started drinking before he even came out to gamble tonight.

"It's good to be home," he says, reaching the bed and turning around. The coyote straightens up and brushes me off. He tries to sit on the bed but misses and ends up on the floor next to the bed with a yelp.

Damn it! "Are you okay?" I ask.

He shrugs. "Maybe I should have quit drinking earlier."

I debate picking him up, but if he's going to throw up, I'd rather he throw up on the floor. It's easier to clean the carpeting than the mattress. I glance around the room to quickly see how he's been holding up in here.

Most things are neat, except for the newspaper. On second look, it appears to be opened up to an article about recent House Un-American Committee investigations because I can see the abbreviation HUAC in in the headline. That would explain why he started drinking earlier. The committee is not a fan of Mr. Lopez.

The only oddity appears to be the picture over the bed. He's replaced our desert landscape picture with a painting. Housekeeping had told me this, but it's the first time I've seen it. The canvas contains a picture of a male wolf, leaning in repose in a classical setting, his nude form resting on a pedestal of marble adorned with pillows and fabric. According to Mr. Lopez, the painting is a nineteenth century French piece. It's a nice picture, but just looking at it, I can tell why he's put it up. It's a tasteful piece that has erotic undertones with how immodest the wolf is, smiling at the viewer coyly. It is also the only way he's personalized the room to show that he lives here now.

I glance back down at him. He's just leaning back against the bed with his eyes closed. "Do you need anything else?" I ask him.

"No, no, I'll be fine," he says, opening his eyes to look up at me.

I nod to myself and make a note to tell housekeeping to be prepared to clean the carpet in the morning. I walk over to the door. "Goodnight Mr. Lopez," I say, opening the door.

"Goodnight Antwon," he says, and then before I can close the door, "see you tomorrow."

୬

My little apartment in downtown Vegas is small. The furniture is simple, and the walls are plain adobe, but it's home. I take the opportunity to sleep in and get a call from work in the early afternoon on the party line. I and the downstairs neighbor pick up at the same time. After some pleasantries with Mrs. Walters, I chat briefly with the daytime manager who tells me I was spot on about Mr. Lopez puking on the carpet. I sigh and ask him if I need to keep a better eye on him after he performs.

"It might help. That man drinks more than anyone else," says Jorge. "He's currently regaling some marines in the bar with stories about his performances in the Pacific for the GIs during the war. They're eating it up."

"He's already drinking?" I remark surprised.

"Oh yeah. He's got that girl he's been seeing with him too."

I shake my head. "He drinks, he fucks, he sings. I guess it's the good life."

"The hell if I know," remarks the cougar on the other end of the line. "I'm too busy working to do that. See you Wednesday, Antwon."

"Sounds good," I say hanging up. Mr. Lopez is a horrible lush, but at least he's a good singer. He'd be useless if he wasn't.

My paycheck is sitting on the table by the door, reminding me how much more valuable Mr. Lopez is to the hotel than me. Next to it is a flyer I found on my door a few days ago about tonight's test. I guess I might as well cash the check. It will get me out of the house, and I could use a late lunch.

෨

It's already dark when I return from the store carrying groceries. I hadn't meant to be out so long, but I took care of some other errands. On the front stair, Mrs. Walters intercepts me. The rat flags me down as I'm going inside, a piece of paper in her hands.

"You got a call while you were out," she says, handing it to me.

"Oh, is it work again?" I ask.

"I don't think so. It was a Mr. Lopez asking if you were available. He sounded eager to talk to you and was disappointed you weren't home."

"That's work," I say, taking the piece of paper with his name and a number by it. I immediately recognize the Desert Sun's phone number and his room number on the sheet.

"It was? He said you two were to meet up for dinner."

"I…" I shut my mouth. Mrs. Walters is my downstairs neighbor, but for good reason I don't tell her everything I do. It's better that way. "I forgot that was today. Thank you. I'll give him a call back."

Back upstairs, I put my groceries away in the cupboard and the icebox before I walk over to the phone and ring the hotel via the operator. I get switched over to the hotel's operator who patches me through to Mr. Lopez's room. The phone rings twice before he picks up.

"Jacob Lopez speaking."

"Mr. Lopez, you called earlier?"

"Antwon, yes, yes I did."

"Is there a problem with your room? Jorge should still be on duty and can make sure—"

He cuts me off. "You promised you'd give me a call today, Antwon."

I cough politely and twist my hands around. It's a nervous habit I have to watch at work, but since he can't see me, it doesn't matter. "You were drunk, sir. I didn't think you would remember."

"I remember, and it's Jacob, please. I was hoping to see you off the clock."

What on earth does he want from me? I'm just a concierge. "I see."

"I know it's almost eight, but would you be interested in dinner? I can send a car, if you'd like."

"I have my own, but why?"

I get a little burst of static on the line just then; I think because he's idly playing with the cord. "You're an honest man, Antwon. One of the few at the Sun who looks past the facade."

I'm losing my patience, so I let him have it. "Mr. Lopez. Sorry, Jacob. You were drunk. It's not hard to look past the sweet voice and see that." I pause, and when he doesn't say anything, I continue. "And if I may be so bold, you're on your way to being a washed-up singer. It's not the job, it's the way you carry yourself that suggests it. Your legal troubles back east are well known."

There isn't an immediate response. I wonder if I've pushed back too far, but then there is a chuckle. "It's an accurate assessment. You see past the facade and what's really there. I had hoped getting out of New York for a while would help, but it hasn't. So, dinner? I can come pick you up if you give me the address."

I'm forced now to think, sorting out how the coyote acts to try and understand why he's asking me to eat with him. I maintain the highest standard of professionalism I can, but I've slipped up a few times. What Joanna said last night might be it, but I've never spoken to Mr. Lopez about my affairs. If that's not it, I'm drawing up a blank.

"Antwon?"

"Is your girlfriend going to be there?" It's worth stalling for a minute.

He chuckles. "I'm fairly sure you know she won't be there. It's just us."

Just us? The plot thickens. Someone has told the coyote the swift fox in the dark suit up front isn't exactly what he makes himself out to be.

"Please?" he adds softly.

There's something in the one word request, a sense of vulnerability that becomes crystal clear the moment he says it. It's the request of someone alone in this world.

"All right… Jacob. Pick me up at nine. I know a small place we can talk you won't be recognized in."

჻

An hour later a blue Buick Special sedan with a white hard top pulls up outside under the streetlamp. I recognize it from the Desert Sun's parking lot. Jacob doesn't get out of the car, so I go down after locking the front door. Mrs. Walters doesn't come out to say anything to me. Her husband must have just got home from an evening shift in the rail yard. I walk around the car and get in.

"Hey," says the coyote, as I slip onto the bench seat. The inside is comfortable with a chrome dash and a soft bench seat. The material is a nice gray, so it doesn't clash with the outside. The radio is on, playing some song that was big during the war. I see Mr. Lopez is well dressed with a nice suit and tie. The jacket is on the back seat. I've taken a more comfortable approach with a button up shirt open at the top to let my chest fluff breathe.

"I'm here," I say. "Why did you want to get dinner?" Party lines aren't always the most private, so before we let this evening begin, I'd like to see what he says.

"Do you have to be so formal all the time?" he responds, as he backs the car up and then pauses. "Where are we going anyway?"

The big engine rumbles as the car sits in the middle of the road. "To the first question, I'm not the one who wore a suit. To the second, that kind of depends on why I'm here."

Jacob scratches at an ear. "Yeah. I guess. Is there a good diner nearby?"

I motion. "Yes. Go up three blocks and then take a left. I walk there when it's not too hot out."

He shifts the car in gear. "All right. In answer to your question, well I said you deserved a day off."

"I'm shocked you remembered the exchange. You were quite inebriated."

"I have to remember a lot of things from when I'm drunk. I've gotten good at it."

"Perhaps," I offer, "you should drink less. You're not a very good gambler when you're drunk."

He grumbles and we ride on in silence as he makes the left and goes up a block. We pass a Civil Defense truck going in the opposite direction before pulling into the diner. He kills the car engine and then turns to look at me.

"My agent tells me that already. I'd be a lot better off if I drank a little less and hit the poker table less, but why shouldn't I enjoy my exile? Surely you can't be so uptight, Antwon, to deny a man his pleasures?"

"Of all people, you know I'm not one to do that. I just don't understand is all. You had everything going for you. Everything all lined up."

"Sometimes we hate the gilded cages we're forced to live in. I've seen yours, so don't judge me for not liking my own," he says, opening the door and getting up. I follow suit and we look at each other over the top of the car. I should say something about how I don't live in a cage, but it's astute of him to notice how my actions at work are carefully planned.

"Not all of us can afford to fall like you did, and not hit the ground."

"I used to think I hadn't hit it, but maybe I just didn't realize I did." He shrugs. "Come on, my treat," he says, pointing his thumb toward the door. "I'll tell you the story of why I'm out here."

We walk in and take seats at the counter. The diner is bright with chrome fixtures. There are customers, but it's not busy. "I've heard it already. It's not like it hasn't been floating around with the rest of the staff," I remark.

The coyote chuckles and wags. "There are a few stories about you floating around back there. They're just not as exciting as mine."

"Is that what brought you to ask me to get dinner?"

He leans over to whisper into my ear. "A little, but I had you peeped, foxy, before I heard about your fling with the bartender from San Francisco. They say you were really upset when he went back to California. I remember when he left the week after I came in from the east."

I growl and whisper back, "Mr. Lopez, I don't think we should be having this conversation here."

"No? The pie in the case over there looks amazing. We can talk about how life has treated us like crap over a slice."

I breathe in and out to steady my shaking nerves. "This isn't the place."

"Don't be so stuck up, Antwon. What is there for you to lose?"

"My job." That waitress is still busy helping someone else so we've got a minute. "I know you came out here to lay low after you got caught with some rent boy."

Just then, the waitress walks up and gave us a look over. The ocelot doesn't seem too impressed. "What are you boys having?"

"Cheeseburger, fries, a cup of coffee, and a slice of pie," says Jacob, unfazed by what I just said. "Antwon?"

"Uh... the same."

"Sounds good," says the ocelot, walking away to give our order to the short order cook.

"Chester," says Jacob, "is not a rent boy. We had a good run. It wouldn't have been an issue but they were already keeping an eye on him because he had friends who were communists. They tracked him down to my place, and when they realized they had a pair of homosexuals, well, they're automatically subversives. It didn't matter who I was."

I blink, taking a moment to digest what he said before I move to get up. "Look, I'm going to go. I can walk home."

"Please don't," he says, as a hand catches my arm.

"I don't understand how you can be so callous about other people's safety."

Jacob chuckles. "Safety, huh? You're what, twenty-seven?"

"Actually, it's twenty-six."

"I'm thirty-seven. You're two years too young to understand."

It takes me a minute. "You mean I was too young to fight in the war?"

"Yup."

I've heard his war story already. "You were in a Special Services entertainment unit."

"Yup."

I smirk. "It was a cushy job."

He growls, annoyed, and leans over to get closer to me. "Yeah, real cushy." He shakes his head at me. "I was on one DC-3 that got hit while trying to land in the Pacific. The Japs decided it was a good time to attack the airbase. The starboard side engine caught fire, and we lost the wing when we hit the ground. The pilot kept her on the runway though and put her down. All of the Special Service personal onboard walked away bruised. The pilot died later from his injuries."

I'm not sure what I should say. "I didn't know," is all I can muster.

He shrugs. "I spent three and a half years near the front line being a beacon of hope for our boys in uniform. Their tired faces would light up when I stepped out on stage. They needed the brief respite our little performance could give them, and I gave them my all. Coming home after the war, everything I did felt cheap. So, when Korea came up three years ago, I went over there with the U.S.O. and did two tours. All of it didn't mean a damn thing though when I got outed."

"You're at least proud of what you did?" I offer.

"I am, but look what happened. We fought a war to stop a madman in Europe, and now we have a new madman in Europe. Korea is just a proxy war for a bigger conflict that's developing."

The waitress comes over with our coffee and drops it off. Jacob picks it up and takes a sip. I can tell the fur on my tail has bristled. I use this moment to interject. "Whatever happens in Europe, we'll be safe over here. The work they're doing out in the desert tonight is to help make us safer."

"Safe?" he laughs mirthlessly. He puts the cup down. "You think that's going to make us safe? All we're doing is creating a culture of fear. They're teaching school children back east how to duck and cover under their desks in the event of a nuclear attack."

"Mutually assured destruction—"

He slams his fist down on the counter. "It's a death cult. All of this is a fucking death cult!"

The people in the diner are staring at us. Jacob glances around, sighs, and picks up his coffee.

"You should learn some respect for the people in uniform," says a wolf down the counter.

Jacob twists his face into a contorted glare, so I intervene before he can say something.

"He did support work during both of the last wars."

The wolf glares at Jacob. "Oh?"

"Yeah. I helped entertain the troops and visited the wounded in the hospital. I saw a lot of maimed soldiers over there. I even got to go to Japan after the war. I saw what happens in a city when you drop one of those bombs on it."

The wolf gives the coyote a glare before he turns back to his plate of food. "Just show some respect. They're trying hard to keep us safe."

Jacob sighs and slumps forward. He stares at his black coffee for a minute before he whispers something to me. "It's not the people I'm judging."

"You saw what happened in Japan?" I inquire.

"Yeah, my last Special Services tour of the second world war was with the occupation force. Miles of city flattened and burned into nothing."

I could say that we did it to save our own people, that the Japanese were going to fight to the last man, but it doesn't change the fact that we developed this weapon. We're the ones who used it first and unleashed this horror. And now, we're not the only ones who have it. Even I know that seeing all that devastation and knowing about the death that went with it changes a man. There isn't anything I can say to that.

Thankfully, the waitress comes back with our food, and we eat in silence. Jacob chews slowly, looking lost in thought. When he finishes he gets the check and pays. He gives the waitress a ten dollar bill and tells her to keep the change on a meal that costs under five dollars. She gushes over herself when he does.

"Ready?" he asks me after she's walked over to the register.

"Yeah," I respond. He gets up, and so I do, following him outside. He walks up to the car and turns around waiting for me before I ask, "Where are we going?"

He shrugs, perky canine ears dropping. "I figured I burned off all my good will, so I'll drop you back home?"

"I guess."

He gets into the car and reaches across to unlock the door. I slide in. Just before he starts the car, I ask him the question that's burning in my mind. "Why did you let them catch you?"

He flicks an ear. "With Chester?"

"Yeah. You're not the only fairy out there, but you're certainly one of the better known now. Why did you let them catch you in the act?"

"Some of what you've heard is likely overblown. We weren't doing it, but I also didn't bother to protest either. Frankly, I don't care. I did a lot for this country, and if they don't like it, well, fuck them."

"But your career?"

He laughs. "Fuck that asshole in the senate. He wants to call me a 'sexual pervert' now, huh? Well, I'd like to shove something up him and the House Un-American Activities Committee. We both know homosexuality isn't a sickness of the mind. I may not get another record cut for a long time, but it doesn't matter here in Las Vegas. The mob built this city, and as long as I stay clean of them, a sexual pervert like me is fine here."

"I know you're lying," I say, leaning in the seat so I can get a better look at him. "Your drinking shows it bothers you."

He puts the key into the ignition. "I'm just trying to make sure my detractors get a chance to come to my funeral."

"What about Chester?"

He pauses shifting gears. "Chester's dead. He took a necktie and hung himself."

"Oh…"

"Any other questions before I take you back, foxy?"

I rest my hand on his shoulder. "Sorry."

The coyote shifts the car into gear. "It's okay. I'm a mess. I'm just trying not to let everyone know."

"Everyone who works for the hotel knows."

He sucks in his breath as he turns onto the main street. "Yeah, I shouldn't drink so much. In my defense, there is not a lot to do out here. I don't have any friends here, just some acquaintances. I get a few letters from New York, and I talk to my agent once a week. That's the extent of my social circle."

"I understand the feeling of isolation. It's why I was so upset when Bret went back to San Francisco."

He pulls up to my apartment and turns the car off. "If it meant so much to you, why didn't you go with him?"

It's my turn to feel flustered. "It wasn't that way. We were good together, but it was also convenience."

"Yeah, it's not easy to meet guys. I'm still trying to learn how you do that out here. Any tips?"

I smile. "For starters, don't drop all your emotional baggage on someone when you first get to talk to them."

He puts a paw on his chest. "It's been building up for a while."

"Next, I would suggest drinking less."

"Okay, that's a given."

"Finally, work on your approach."

He scratches behind his ears. "So no going to the city park after dark?"

"You've done that?" I respond shocked.

He nods. "Yeah… a tip there if you ever undertake such an endeavor, make sure they're not a police officer first."

"How are you not in jail?" I ask him.

He holds up his hands and shrugs. "My agent has good connections. I know how to talk my way out of a pinch."

"You're not as smooth as you give yourself credit for," I say, shaking my head at him.

He gives me a toothy smirk. "No? You're still in my car."

It's true. I haven't moved to leave yet either. Jacob, for annoying as he is, is the only gay I know in the entire city of Las Vegas right now. I know there are others, but I haven't got any way to meet them. I'm not brave enough to go cruising, and the city isn't that big.

"I'm not rude, you know, but if we just sit here, the lady who lives downstairs with her husband will notice."

"That must make dating difficult."

My tail curls a little tighter, and my ears fall. "Dating?"

"Cocksucking? Whatever you want to call it."

I cough. "We're still coworkers."

"Yeah. Well, thank you for the evening and listening. It wasn't what I had in my head, but I was quite drunk when I suggested it."

Finally, an admission of why I know we're here. "Which is?" I press.

His ears fall. He holds up one paw and makes a circle with it while he sticks a finger through the hole.

"Us, do that?" I say, bringing a hand to my chest. "Mr. Lopez, I'm ashamed you'd think about that. I am a very discreet fox."

He flicks his ears. "Sorry," the coyote mumbles.

"For starters, my neighbors would certainly hear that."

His ears flick and he gives me a confused look. "What?"

"You heard me," I say. "I'm always discreet."

A hand comes to rest on my tail. "How discreet?"

I don't flinch at the intimate touch. Instead, I smile, showing a little fang. "Discreet enough to not get caught. That's why we're not going back to the Desert Sun."

He scratches behind his ear. "Tonight isn't a good night for a deserted street either. With the test tonight, all of the Civil Defense personal are out running drills."

"Perhaps one of the less prestigious hotels in town. There's an older hotel called the Californian off Freemont Street that rents by the hour and takes long term loggers. It's rough and tumble, but it would work. They've been trying to close it for years."

He wrinkles his nose. "I prefer the car. The last time I was in one of those places, I got fleas. What about just driving out of town? There has to be deserted highway out there."

"I know a good place up near Mt. Charleston. There's a scenic overlook, and it should be deserted. It's only a forty-five minute drive."

"Sure, it sounds good, foxy," he says putting the key into the ignition. The engine purrs to life. "A drive would do me some good."

"Yeah," I say settling back against the seat. The car pulls back out and turns, heading west. Maybe I'm mad for suggesting this and still being here, but I also need the company.

৯

The lights of Las Vegas had faded behind us quite a while ago by the time we turn onto Route 157 and follow the road through a canyon up into the mountains. I let the worry we might be seen go, and I allow myself to lean against Jacob as he drives up the twisting highway.

The coyote woofs when I lean against him, and I can feel his tail wag against the seat as he steers the Buick. It's a relaxing drive, and the sky is clear with stars covering the landscape. He has the windows cracked and once we reach the tree line and enter the national forest, the smell of pine filters into the car. We don't encounter any cars as we head up into the forest. There are no lights either out here, just the car's headlights.

The radio plays softly, the station playing different standards that have been popular in the last ten years. It's already quite late, so about thirty minutes in the announcer comes on the air and does the nightly sign-off. Afterward, there is just dead air on the radio.

"Since it's a clear night, we should be able to pick up one of the twenty-four hour LA stations," I say, adjusting the knob on the radio.

"We should be able to," he replies, steering the Buck around a curve.

After a minute, I pick one up playing jazz. I settle back against the coyote, watching the road. Shortly afterward, he reaches a junction in the road and turns off of it. Even though it's clear, it's so late I can only make out one of two lights from the village at the base of Mt. Charleston.

Ten minutes later a brown sign comes up in the headlights. "This is it," I say, and he pulls over at the Desert View Overlook. The parking lot is completely deserted.

"This is really remote," he says. "We're far more likely to encounter one of our wild ancestors than a person out here."

"Hey, it's discreet," I say leaning my muzzle up to lick the side of his face in the glow of the radio dial.

He kills the car and turns to look at me. It's a clear, moonless night out. There's no one out here besides us. We are truly alone. I have good night vision, but in the low light, he's just a colorless shadow against me.

He rubs an arm against my shoulder, I can feel his pinned tail trying to wag. "I like this, actually."

"Good," I say tracing a paw across the hem of his shirt.

He chuckles and slips a hand to my chest to undo the top button of my shirt.

I pull away from him for a moment. "You know, we don't have to do it in here. The top of the overlook isn't that far away."

"Oh!" He chuckles. "That would be different. You've done this before haven't you?"

"Bret and I came out here once, but he didn't want to leave the car. He found it too primal for his taste."

I can see Jacob loosening his necktie and undoing the buttons on his shirt. "Primal doesn't bother me," he says and then leans forward to kiss me. His breath is warm against mine, his tongue wet in my muzzle. "It's nice to remember where we've come from."

I press a hand to his chest and tug at his half undone necktie before I let him go. "Then come on." I'm already feeling flush from anticipation.

"Sure," he says, scooting back across the bench seat so he can get out of the car. I follow suit.

Outside, the air is cool, a soft breeze on the air. The heat from the day has faded away, although the pavement is still warm to the pads on my feet.

"Lead on," the coyote says. I do, and as soon as I set out on the path, I can feel the coyote behind me, gently holding onto my tail like a pup.

"Worried about getting lost," I ask, turning back to glance at him.

His tail wags. "Last time I had sex was in New York. I don't want to let the opportunity escape from me."

I chuckle. He's cute when he's playful like this. I lead him up the trail to the overlook on top of the mountain. From up here, you can see for miles away. The mountains and valleys are shrouded in the deep cloak of night. The lights of Las Vegas are hidden to the east by the mountains leaving only feeble starlight to outline the ridge tops.

I feel hands wrap around me. "It's a nice view."

I turn to look at the coyote, my thick fox brush tail rubbing against him. "The mountains, or me from the rear?"

"Both?"

I chuckle. "So, tell me, Mr. Lopez. How do you like your homosexuality? Is it a top or bottom thing for you?"

"Hmm." He thinks. "I'm partial to the ass, but I'm also partial to the cock. It depends on my mood."

I give my tail a swish as I tug my shirt hem out of my pants. "Well, what about tonight?"

He wraps his hands around my waist and licks at my muzzle. "Let's keep it simple tonight."

"Why, you think I can't do complex?" I whisper into his right ear.

I feel his paws reaching down to grip my rump. "You're such a proper fox." I feel a finger tracing at the cleft of my ass. "I don't think you are a messy kind of guy."

I make a satisfied rumble in my chest and kiss the side of his muzzle. "There is a certain kind of stickiness I do enjoy." I reach up to remove his shirt. He pulls his hands out of my pants, and lets me undress him. When I get it halfway down, I pull it against him, pinning his arms against his sides. "Now, who has been a very bad yote?"

He lets his tongue roll and gives me a goofy grin. "You know a good coyote?"

"I know a few who can keep themselves out of the national news."

He laughs and wiggles. "Want me to show you why I'll never be a respectable singer again?" He brushes the front of my pants with one of his hands. Already I can feel I'm straining against the fabric. I haven't had sex since Bret left town, and I definitely have my own feelings of urgency.

I let go of his shirt, and it falls to the ground. "Sure, let's see what else you can do with that honey-tinged muzzle of yours."

He gets down on his knees and slowly pulls my belt open with his muzzle. Deft fingers undo my zipper and pull down my drawers, exposing me to the cool night air and hot coyote breathe. He pants and gently noses around my shaft with his cold nose, getting it hard and out of its sheath.

I shiver and Jacob brings a paw up to hold me steady as he gently licks up and down the shaft, careful not to graze me with his sharp teeth. He has a relaxed attitude to sex. He's got my shaft nice and wet just by tonguing at it before he even takes it into his muzzle.

"Do you always play with your toys?" I ask him.

He glances up at me, my cock in his mouth, and gives me a quizzical expression, one ear up, and one ear down. I read the innocent, "me, do that?" look he's conveying while he's proceeding to do exactly what I just accused him of. A clawed finger against my pucker is suddenly added to the mix. As he begins to bob on my shaft, he's also exploring the area under my tail.

The tightness in my rear confirms it's been a while, but Jacob works me to loosen me up. I also don't give him much air, keeping his head down, muzzle on my shaft. Unfortunately, our needs are too great to undertake the penetration the coyote's finger suggests, because my knot quickly swells. Jacob has to break off probing me in order to play with himself, although he doesn't stop sucking. One paw rests around my shaft to keep me steady as he bobs.

All too quickly, I feel myself let go and he pulls back surprised. My cum splashes down onto his throat and belly. Sitting back, he starts to jerk himself harder until he also comes. Some of it tags my leg, but the rest hits the ground.

"Oh god, it's been too long," he says, panting in the darkness with me.

I step around him, and I can feel my knees get weak. "It's been a while for me too," I say, sitting down next to him. Exhaustion is starting to hit me now. It's been a busier day than I expected.

"Maybe we should come up here again," he suggests.

I feel my tail wag against the ground. "I wouldn't be averse to that."

We rest on the ground next to each other for a few minutes. I close my eyes, just enjoying the company. We're still in that position when there is a brilliant flash so bright that even with my eyes closed, I can see it. I try and open my eyes to see what the source of the luminosity is, but the flash is all consuming. For a moment I'm confused and disoriented in a sea of white light.

"What the hell!" yells Jacob. I can hear him scrambling around next to me, bumping into me.

The light starts to fade, and then it hits me. "It's the test." I realize and scramble to my feet. "Look!" I yell, pointing.

In the distance beyond the valley below and behind a ridge line, a giant ball of fire is rising up from the desert floor. As it begins to fade, it takes on the shape of a mushroom cloud. It's the atomic test scheduled for tonight on the Nevada Test Site.

Jacob sucks in his breath. "I forgot that was tonight," he whispers, ears back. He's on his feet, ears swept back in a panicked way.

"Yeah," I say. "Me too. I got distracted."

He shivers noticeably, his body shaking.

"Are you okay?" I say, turning to him. We're both naked and the light has already faded away, leaving a strange air of nothingness in its place. The distant cloud is losing its luminosity now.

"I never thought I'd be so close to an atomic detonation. All of that destructive power."

"It's okay. I've seen them from downtown Las Vegas before. We're safe."

He turns away, tail between his legs. His whole body quivers.

"Hey," I say, wrapping an arm around him. He lurches forward, and I have to catch him as he sinks to his knees. "Oh god, are you going to be okay?"

He turns to me, his naked body trembling. "I just, I'm remembering what I saw in Japan."

I hug him to me. The coyote's violently shaking against me. "It will be okay," I say, gently stroking his naked shoulders.

"Will it be?" he whispers. "Can we trust our leaders not to do something stupid? They're already looking to flush every communist and homosexual they can find out of government in some glorious crusade against the Russians. It's not because these people are dangerous, it's just so they can have someone to be the fall guy. They need an enemy. People always need an enemy if they want to unite. In the war it was the Nazis and the Japanese. Now it's the communists."

I look out across the desert. The light has faded. Against the moonless, starlit landscape I just barely see the shape of the mushroom cloud. "We can only hope that in the face of such power, such danger, that we as a people can be stronger, less animalistic than our ancestors. Nor can you hold the weight of the world on your shoulders. It will crush you as surely as if you were a grape. Only together can we lift the ship."

His voice is weak. "It means little in the face of total, utter annihilation."

I sigh. "We're still here today, and we should be here tomorrow."

He whispers. "And after that?"

"I guess we'll have to see." I rub his back gently. He's naked and splattered with my cum, but the sex we just had has been forgotten.

He exhales deeply and rests a hand against the ground. "Ashes to ashes. Dust to dust." He gently runs a paw across the earth. "We are born from this land, and when we die, we return to it. Why is it so hard for people to see beyond themselves and think of the pack?"

"I don't know, but I understand your frustration. We're all trying to survive. Why must people hold each other back?"

He doesn't say anything, but he just stares at the ground for a bit. I wait, and finally he looks up at me. "Do you think me mad?"

"Mad? No. You're hurt, and I can see that. No one is going to pull you out of this but yourself."

"Sometimes I wish I was more of a man than I am."

I get close to him so he can't look away. "I haven't seen what you've seen, but I realize it doesn't sit right with you. I can see the stress, but it's something you have to work to come to terms with."

"It's weird that the homosexuality is what most people think is wrong with me. They don't see the real me," he says wistfully.

"I do now. I've seen more of who you are today than I've seen in the last two months. This has not exactly been the type of hookup I go for, but it's shown me the real you."

He pushes himself up to stand tall. The cloak of night wraps itself around him, but he holds out a hand. The scent of our bodies drifts across the breeze, and I can smell the results of our lovemaking on him. "I guess that's something. I at least got you out of your shell tonight."

I chuckle and take his offered hand, and he pulls me up. "You did. Perhaps I can help pull you out of yours next."

༄

The hum of the car has relaxed me so much that I must have dozed off at some point. The radio is playing, but I stopped paying attention a while back. Both Jacob and I have been quiet during the drive back to Las Vegas. "Do you know what this is?" he asks me, waking me up from my exhausted stupor.

I lift my head from where I had it on his shoulder. Even though I've dressed, I'm going to need a shower to get his scent off of me. Jacob isn't any better, and I can feel where the fur on his stomach has become dried and matted under one of my paws. There is a slight earthy smell in the air, though, and it's overtaking the other scents in the car.

I look out over the hood of the car. The lights of Vegas are in the distance now, since we've come out of the mountains and are driving across the valley floor. Jacob is squinting at the road where in the light of the headlights a light pink dust seems to be falling out of the air. The particles are very fine, but you can see the slight haze they make in the headlights.

"Yeah," I say. "It happens sometimes after they do the tests. The government says it's not dangerous, but it's fallout from the test."

He squints at the dust as the car drives through it. "Does this make it into the city?"

"It's happened once, but usually it's to the north of town. It's hardly noticeable and blows away quickly."

He reaches and rolls up the window, which he had cracked again. "If you don't mind, I would prefer to keep the windows up."

"Sure." I stretch and move to my side of the car and close the other window. Then I yawn and curl back up against him. Up ahead, in the distance, I can see the lights of Las Vegas, glowing in the distance. Jacob rests an arm against me. I snuggle against him, enjoying his scent and warmth. The world is a scary place, but in this moment, I'm not thinking of that or how it might end. Only the coyote is on my mind.

There may be a tough road ahead for us all in the world if they keep building new atomic weapons, but I have faith no one will push the button. It may be naïve on my part, but hope is all we have sometimes. You'd have to be beyond mad to use one anyway.

Published in Heat #16 *back in 2019 by Sofawolf Press, this story required quite a bit of research to write. There are a lot of technical aspects in this that I tried touch on to give the story life, while also not bogging it down in aircraft operations.*

Mile High

"50, 40, 30, 20… 10…" called the automatic voice.

With a gentle bump, I got the back wheels of the plane down on the tarmac and lowered the nose. The autobrake engaged and my first officer, the tiger next to me, gave me a thumbs up as we slowed down.

"Yankee-foxtrot-six-six-niner, *bienvenue en Guadeloupe,* exit right on bravo, contact ground one-two-one decimal eight-five for taxi," came the voice over the headset.

Finally, we had arrived at our last destination of the day. I would have tried to wag my bushy fox tail, but it was pinned against the seat. Donovan just watched the instrument panels quietly, not bothering to talk, although I noticed his tail tip was twitching. After slowing down, we took the taxiway to the general aviation ramp. The next twenty minutes were spent following ground controller instructions until the plane was parked and shut down. Once it was all done and we completed our checklist, we were free till the next morning.

"I'm excited to see someplace new," said Bettie Jane, our flight attendant, as we walked off the tarmac.

I just made a noncommittal noise in response, worn from the long day.

"I'm glad we're finally here," Donovan said, his tail lashing in excitement.

The ground crew were friendly, although I think we kind of made a weird sight. Donovan was the tall and stocky tiger while I was the short and slender swift fox. Bettie Jane, a racoon, fell in the middle between us. Swift foxes aren't known for their height, so I couldn't blame the raccoon for being taller than me, but I still wished I had a few more inches. At least my big ears helped me look taller.

After we chatted with the ground crew for a bit, they called us a cab to take us to our hotel. They and the hotel staff were the only people I expected to encounter this trip that spoke English.

"How is your French?" Donovan asked Bettie Jane.

"I know a little," said the raccoon, grinning.

The tiger clicked his tongue. "Only a little? Why, you will barely be able to order an aperitif, let alone a full meal!"

"The hotel has bilingual staff," I said.

"Having come all this way, are we not going to explore?" replied Bettie Jane.

I glanced at my watch. It read 6:45, but that was set to EST. We were a time zone ahead now. "I'd like to get some rest before tomorrow's flight. It's a long trip to New York, and we pick up our passenger at 9 AM."

"Oh, come on. Some play time before bed will be fine," said Bettie. "You're far too uptight for a fox, Jonas."

Donovan added, "Where is your sense of adventure?"

I huffed, annoyed. I preferred if they went off on their own. What I needed I couldn't get with them around anyway. Bettie Jane's bubbliness tended to get on my nerves when I was overtired. And Donovan? It was my first trip with him since he joined the company six months ago, and I personally didn't like him now that I'd flown with him. He was bossy, twitchy, and kept trying to tell me what to do even though I was the captain and he was only the first officer. "I'm honestly tired," I said, as the cab pulled up to take us to the hotel.

"*C'est vous, les Américains?*" asked the driver, rolling down the passenger window.

"*Oui,*" said Donovan.

The driver, a leopard, gave us all a nod and got out to load our luggage into the trunk. Bettie got in the front, while Donovan and I got in the back. Once everyone was seated, he took off toward downtown, not even asking where we were going. The guy who called the cab for us spoke French over the phone, so I assumed the driver didn't speak English. I tried to follow along as the car headed down the street and merged onto a small highway, but after a couple of traffic circles, I was hopelessly lost.

"Oh hey, does your cell-phone do international roaming?" Donovan asked. "Mine is only domestic."

"Yeah," I said, fishing it out of my pocket. "Let me turn it on first."

"Thanks. I've been meaning to get an international plan, but most of my flights have been domestic."

"It comes in handy. Here you go," I said, unlocking it and handing it to him.

"Awesome," the tiger replied, punching in a number, and then put the receiver to his ear after extending the muzzle mic. It rang once or twice, and someone picked up. He said, "Hi Mom!" and I tuned him out. I just watched the houses go by as we cruised through Pointe-à-Pitre. We passed small apartment blocks of three to four stories as we drove through the city, with squat, older row houses interspersed. The hotel the company sprang for wasn't a beachfront place, so we didn't go through any of the more touristy areas.

"Here you go," said Donovan a few minutes later, handing back my phone. "Thank you!"

I tucked it into my slacks. "No problem." The car pulled off the small highway we had been going down, went through another traffic circle to connect to a side road, and then pulled into the entrance of our destination. We piled out of the cab along with our luggage.

The hotel was a little way out of downtown, where the apartments had given way to houses. Donovan suggested it, and he was very insistent we stay there. He argued with corporate saying he had a friend who stayed there last year, and it was well within budget. I would have voiced an opinion, but the price was reasonable enough. I didn't expect to have any time to explore with us getting to the hotel at 8 PM local time. That gave us a little under twelve hours before we needed to be back in a cab to arrive at the airport by 8 AM.

The two-story main building was surrounded by small bungalows and well-manicured grounds trimmed with lush vegetation. There was a cute pool and a hotel restaurant with a bar. It was a resort, but not an expensive one. Still, it was a welcome break from some of the places I've stayed in. Flying private charters, the hotels are nicer, the clientele is much fussier, but the hours are only marginally better when compared to flying for an airline.

I was not surprised that, after getting the rooms, Donovan offered to take Bettie into Pointe-à-Pitre to show her some local cuisine.

"You absolutely must come with me to downtown for dinner. We can go see the old colonial houses down there too. We'll leave the stuffy fox behind. He doesn't want to explore anyway."

I rolled my eyes. "Just watch your time," I advised them.

"*Oui monsieur,*" Donovan said to me, as he walked off to have the hotel staff arrange a cab to be waiting for them after they dropped their luggage in their rooms. I watched him with a scowl. Something about him wasn't right, but I couldn't put my finger on it. Finally, I shook my head and headed up to my own room. I would tell corporate when I got back to NYC not to pair us together again.

๛

After changing out of my uniform, I went down to the restaurant wearing a Hawaiian shirt. Bettie Jane and Donovan weren't in the lobby when I walked through it, so I assumed they were already gone. The restaurant was nicely appointed with rich brown wood, white tablecloths, and a palm tree motif. I opted to sit at the bar, nursing a ginger ale because it at least made me feel like I was drinking something strong. I was tired, I really wanted a good drink, but it was a little too close to my morning flight for a whiskey on the rocks. The menu turned out to be a collection of various Caribbean dishes, and after going over it, I ordered the curry chicken since it intrigued me, wondering how it differed from an Indian curry chicken.

I sighed as I finished the soda off and put it down. I pondered if I should squeeze in a good beer. There were some on the menu that sounded interesting, and it would have given me something else to do while I waited for my food. Bored, I pulled out my phone to go over tomorrow's itinerary. We were scheduled to be picking up a single passenger in the morning, a Mr. Charles Danforth, and take him to New York. I had no idea who Mr. Danforth was, but the fact he paid for a solo flight for himself struck me as odd. An international charter service like this for a single person was not cheap. After Mr. Danforth, we were to shuttle a group of eight to Washington DC and return a different group to New York City. Then I would be home for three days before I flew out again.

Satisfied with tomorrow's itinerary, I put the phone back down. The moment I did it buzzed, and I picked it back up, annoyed. I saw a message just saying, *Hello,* on there. I squinted at it and swiped down, surprised to see I left Barked running.

165

I swore I turned it off before I started this trip. There is little point to use it when I'm flying; most of the time my phone is off, but it's especially useless in a country where most people don't speak the only language I know.

To my surprise though, the person who hit me up, YenaBoy45721, is an American who the service said was nearby in Guadeloupe. A friendly looking spotted hyena smiled at me from the little photo on my screen. A quick glance through his photo gallery told me he was into astronomy and arcade games. There were no crotch shots either in his gallery, which is a plus if you want more than a quick hookup.

Hi, I typed in and hit send. Flirting at least gave me something to do, and I hated always being the responsible one. A little teasing would be fun.

I got a response back quickly that said, *How are you?*

Tired. I pondered for a minute how friendly I was feeling. I glanced down the bar. The bartender was polishing a glass, and a few patrons were talking among themselves. I technically was not alone, but effectively I was by myself. Unless I stayed up and waited for them, I wouldn't see Donovan or Bettie Jane until the morning. I deleted what I had just entered. *Maybe a little lonely. How about you?* I typed in instead and then hit send.

The response came quickly. *I'm good, and I can help you with that.*

Ah, this one is direct. I was hoping for at least a chase. *I'm sure you can, but I'll be fine,* I typed and sent.

I don't want this to be creepy, but you don't look fine from here, sitting at the bar alone.

What? I stopped and looked up. Glancing over my shoulder, I saw a spotted hyena holding up a phone, smiling at me sheepishly. He looked just like the photo of YenaBoy45721. He was in the back of the restaurant at a table. I glanced down at the picture on my phone and back up to confirm. I realized if I had location services turned on, it would have been clear he was physically close to me, instead of being just nearby.

The game was getting interesting. Well, I won't be alone, I said to myself as I got up. I motioned to the bartender where I was going and walked over to the table, carrying my empty drink glass. In moments like that, a good swish of my tail helps seal the deal, but I didn't want to appear that needy. I didn't know anything about this guy, so I wanted to take it slow.

"Sorry, was that too forward of me?" asked the hyena, as I approached him.

"I didn't expect anyone here to hit me up. I have no idea how many people use Barked locally." The tag line of "Hot tails and muzzles barkchained for discreet hookups" pulled in a flirty group of people. Definitely a good group if you're looking to play, not the best group when it came to potential boyfriend material.

"I was just idly looking, and I realized the cute guy at the bar was on here," he said, holding up his phone.

I chuckled. "Cute, but tired guy at the bar." I hadn't sat down yet, as I pondered if I wanted to let the chase be more than a chase.

The hyena's ears fell back a little. "I mean that as, well… just company would be fine. Honest!" he stammered out.

I tilted my head.

"No hookup needed."

That convinced me at least to sit down. In hindsight, things might have turned out differently had I gone back to the bar.

"Jonas," I said, holding out my hand.

"Chuck," he said, taking my hand. "Glad to help brighten your evening."

"Thanks. It's been a long day."

"Rough vacation?" he asked.

"Oh, this isn't a vacation for me. I'm a pilot. I have a morning flight out."

"Oh! I thought with the Hawaiian shirt you were a tourist. It's the same one in your profile picture."

It *is* the same shirt I'm wearing in my Barked profile pic. That he noticed set me at ease. He wasn't just looking at my assets. "Nah. I just get time for dinner on this trip. What about yourself?"

"Business with a bit of pleasure mixed in," he said.

"Oh, what type of business?"

"Medical research and development."

That brought my attention around. "Wow, that sounds like kind of important work."

"I like to think it is. I work with biomechanics, but I, uh… don't want to talk your head off about that." His ears reddened a little. "I'm prone to talking too much if I'm not careful. Would you like some wine? Being a pilot, you must have a lot of very interesting stories to share," the hyena offered. The waiter found me then and brought my food, setting it down in front of me.

"I don't like to drink on work nights."

"Just one bottle?"

I glanced at my watch. It said 8:50 PM local time. It would be close to the twelve-hour cut off time, but one glass would be through my system quickly. "Just a glass of chenin blanc," I said to the waiter.

"One for me as well."

I then examined the plate of curried chicken served with rice and a side of plantains. I could tell it was Indian inspired, but it was also different. It smelled like an Indian curry, but the spice blend was subtly different. Regardless, it looked and smelled amazing. My stomach rumbled. Lunch had been a quick burger in Savannah before a flight to Ft. Lauderdale and then the shuttle flight to Guadeloupe. "I can wait for you to get your food."

I saw the hyena glance off to the side. "No need. It looks like they're bringing mine now."

The waiter returned with a plate of pork ribs that had a sweet aroma of spices and rum. I had seen the Caribbean Rum Ribs on the menu, and I wished I'd ordered those now. The rich scents of garlic, onion, cumin, and chili pepper from both dishes tickled my nose and made my mouth water.

"Wow that smells great. I'm kind of jealous."

He chuckled. "I'll trade you a rib for a piece of chicken."

"Sure," I said with a wag, and we swapped a little food before we started eating. It proved to be an excellent meal, and the wine mixed well with the curry. While we ate, we chatted about the various parts of the world we had visited. I got to tell a few silly pilot stories. Chuck seemed to have traveled mostly on the east coast of the United States, but he'd been to the Caribbean a couple of times. Soon the meal was finished, the wine drunk, and we were just talking, swapping travel stories.

The waiter eventually came up to bus the table. "Another glass of wine?" he asked me.

"No thank you. Check please," I said, responding automatically.

I saw the hyena wanted to order another glass of wine. He had his hand up, but instead he shook his head, and the waiter walked off with our plates. "I guess that's it for the night then."

I checked the time on my phone. 9:27 PM. I didn't have to be up till 6:30 AM. "I've still got an hour to kill. So, what is it you really want, Chuck?"

He smirked and flashed me some fang. "That depends what you want."

This reminded me I picked up this impromptu date off of a hookup app. "A good night's rest and a good flight out in the morning."

Chuck's ears stayed up, which I took as a good sign. This one might actually be a catch. "You aren't the only one with a morning flight out, but I realize not everyone is up for a quickie." He shrugged. "Thanks for the company though."

"No problem," I said, reaching out to take my bill, but he was quicker than me.

"I've got that," he smiled.

My ears tilted in surprise. "You sure?" I should have told him the bill was on the company's dime, but it was too cute to watch him pay for my meal to tell him otherwise.

"Yeah," he said, putting it with his and placing his credit card on top of them.

If there is one thing I love to see in a guy, it is courtesy. He already had written this off as a meal and nothing more. I glanced at my watch. As long as I get to bed by 11:00, I would be fine. I rarely got to put my foxish charms to work anymore, and tonight seemed like a good time to give it a go again.

"Thank you," I smiled, trying to look as disarming as I could. "If you're interested, I could go for a nightcap."

"I would indeed."

༄

I want to blame the wine for what followed, but it was all me. One glass is hardly enough to get me drunk.

Chuck wanted to come back to my room, and was very insistent on that. I asked him about that, and he said he had some equipment for work he had to take back, and that made the room feel too much like an office for him. Lying next to him as he stroked my tummy through my unbuttoned shirt, I got a moment to think about my actions before I committed to them.

"You really should keep pace on the latest tech improvements," he said. "The recent wars have caused a surge in prosthetics research. Scientists are starting to do some really advanced things."

"It sounds cool, but it's not a topic I'm really interested in."

"So, what interests you outside of flying? Obviously, I'm big on science. I'm also an amateur astronomer."

I pondered. "I don't have anything, really."

He frowned. "Nothing?"

"Being a pilot takes up a lot of time. I used to be big into role playing games like Daggers and Dwarfs, but it's tough keeping up with a group when you fly professionally. My schedule flexes a lot."

"Daggers and Dwarfs is so much fun! Some of my friends and I play after work," he said, as his tail thumped against the bed. "Uh, do you like flying professionally?"

"Yeah. The pay is good. Flying new places keeps things fresh, and I get to travel cheaply."

"So, is it true what they say about pilots? You've got someone in every city?" he asked me.

I laughed. "God no. I mean, I'm no angel now, but I can't keep up like that. My last hookup on Barked was something like six months ago. I like being a picky fox."

I feel a finger worming its way through my stomach fur toward my belt. "A picky fox you say?"

"You did pay for dinner."

He giggled. "Oh, that's all I needed to do?" I felt the belt get tugged from its loop.

"And you weren't a total airhead." And I was bored and lonely? That's not the right thing to say in a situation like that, but I know I thought of it.

He leaned in to give me a lick with his big tongue. "I see."

I smirked and leaned up so I could whisper into his ear. "I like big guys also," I said, slipping a hand to cup him. "You seem well hung."

"Hey, small guys need love to too! The average guy is going to be just average."

I wrapped my arms around him. "Then why don't you show some appreciation to the average guy and plant that big muzzle somewhere warm."

He pulled open my belt and grinned at me, before slipping down my chest to tease at my shaft as he fumbled to remove his pants. His shirt was already on the floor.

I whimpered and relaxed into the pillows. This would be a nice capstone to a hard day of flying during a long week. The musk of aroused, male hyena filled my small hotel room with a pleasant, needy scent.

Chuck was dexterous with his tongue too, and it made me squirm as he washed his hot breath and slick tongue over my cock. I didn't know when the last time I'd gotten a blowjob was, but it had been a while. I enjoyed each tender lick and each nuzzle, as if it was the last of my life. I could feel my fingers curling into the sheets as I bucked into his mouth, a fox in need of release.

All too soon, I was panting hard and moaning, squirming under the attention. He kept pushing me, lick after lick, drool dripping into the fur around my base. Then I felt myself shudder, and I grabbed his head, lifted my hips, and came hard into his mouth.

"Oh fox," I panted, letting go and looking down at him between my legs. He hadn't been expecting me to cum so soon, and drool and jizz were all over my groin. "I got it everywhere."

He licked his muzzle. "Someone was eager."

"It's been a while," I mumbled.

"Perhaps you could return the favor," he said with a grin, a plump rod hanging down between his legs.

I smiled and pushed myself up a little. He knelt over my chest at the top of bed and let me familiarize myself with his equipment. The taste was earthy, with his musk a heavy, enticing scent underneath. I took it slow, opting to enjoy myself, and he only whimpered as I handled him. He was indeed a little bigger than me, as I had guessed.

I licked the tip and then worked my way back while using my paw to keep his girth steady, before I worked up to a nice bobbing motion. I'd never been with a hyena before, but it was all familiar, although I noticed he didn't have a knot.

Chuck got into it of course, and he thrust eagerly to meet my muzzle, and soon I had him moaning and panting. I kept at it, working up and down, until he whined cutely and let loose.

Cum splattered into my muzzle, but I misjudged when I thought he was done, because he left a fine trail across my chest when I let him pull back.

"You are going to need a shower," he said sheepishly.

"That wouldn't be the first," I laughed.

"You want to do anything else?" he asked me.

"I wish. I need to get some sleep," I said, with a yawn. Sex rarely wears me out, but I felt the effects acutely that night. "My body isn't going to let me do more."

He nodded, ears down some. "Uh, you fly in and out of New York a lot?"

"Often. I'm based out of there."

"I'm in New Jersey, perhaps we should meet up some-time?"

"Hit me up on Barked," I suggested. Most of the people I've said something like that to never do, but I thought this one felt serious. I at least wanted to save YenaBoy45721 as a contact, and it would be fun to see him again. Knowing how my schedule tended to ruin all my good prospects, I didn't think it would happen, but I was hopeful it would work out.

He picked up his pants and pulled them on. "I guess I shouldn't stay then."

"If you want, you can sleep here. I need to get up at 6:30 though."

He shook his head. "I would just keep you up, probably. I'll shoot you a message tomorrow."

"Sure."

He got back on the bed and gave me a nice kiss, which I returned warmly, even though my muzzle tasted like hyena. After we exchanged goodbyes, he let himself out to return to his hotel room. I pondered taking a shower then, but I opted to just sponge out some of the stickiness in my fur before falling asleep with the room still smelling like sex. I would shower in the morning. It felt clichéd, but at least I wasn't lonely then, and I slept better than I would have had I not spent the evening with Chuck.

෨

"I don't know what I ate, but I've been throwing up all night. This has to be the worst food poisoning I've ever had."

Standing in the hotel lobby at 7:30 AM with Bettie Jane and Donovan brought the first problem of the day. Bettie looked like she'd been through hell. Her fur was matted, and she smelled like bile. I had flown with Bettie dozens of times, and I had never seen the raccoon look like this. The only thing going right that morning is I received a nice, *Have a good flight*, text from YenaBoy45721 earlier, which I responded to in kind before showering and getting ready.

"Where did you go last night?" I asked Donovan.

"We went to a Caribbean place downtown. I had some fish and she got a shrimp dish. The service was great and it looked really clean. Afterward we walked for a bit until she said her stomach was bothering her. Then we took a cab home."

"Bad shrimp can do it," I said to him. "Let me call dispatch, Bettie. I can see if they can delay the flight."

"We can't delay this flight," said Donovan. "Mr. Danforth paid for a private plane, he's going to expect there to be a private plane on time."

Bettie Jane grimaced. "I can get ready. If you give me a bit, I'll be there just before Mr. Danforth arrives."

"Look, delays happen, and we can't just leave Bettie Jane here in Guadeloupe," I said to both of them.

"I'll be fine," she protested.

I shook my head. "I don't want you getting air sick on Mr. Danforth. I'll just tell him we don't have a flight attendant for this flight—"

"I can get up in-flight once we get over the Atlantic and get him any drinks he needs," Donovan interrupted. "Once we clear the Lesser Antilles, it's open ocean until we reach NYC. The only air traffic control handoffs are Bermuda and then the United States."

I scowled. Why wasn't he going to let me change our departure? "That's something dispatch would have to agree too, and they'd need to book Bettie Jane a flight home."

Donovan glared at me. "I'm sure they'll agree to it, but you can call them on the way to the airport. Come on, we have a plane to get ready, and our cab is here."

I scowled. I was sick of this passive aggressive bullying. "No, we call them first, then we go to the airport," I said pulling out my phone. "As I recall, you don't have international calling on your phone."

❧

I made Donovan wait in the hotel lobby while I spoke to dispatch and went over the option he proposed. They said that would be fine, and they were going to call in a stewardess to meet us after we landed to handle the next two flights of the day. By then, Bettie Jane had run back to her room to throw up again, so I spoke to the front desk to make sure someone

175

would help her and take her to a local hospital. I even went with them to make sure she let them in before I returned to the lobby where Donovan waited. Then and only then, did I get into the cab with Donovan. He glared at me the entire way to the airport, but I didn't care. I wasn't flying with him after this trip if I could help it.

The small business jet sat where we left it, already fueled when we arrived. We went over the weather, did the internal and external inspections with the bare minimum of words and got the plane ready to go. We even had time to stock the mini bar and fluff the pillows, something Bettie Jane would do. Then we waited for our charge to arrive. Donovan got bored and fixed us both seltzer drinks, and I thanked him. It was strangely salty, but I didn't think much of it at the time.

9:00 AM came and went, and it was almost 9:30 when a taxi pulled out onto the tarmac. A spotted hyena dressed in a suit got out and tipped the driver, who started removing a good bit of luggage from the trunk and the backseat.

I came out of the plane. "Mr. Danforth, I'm Captain Jonas Fieldstar. I'll be your pilot for today," I said sticking out my hand.

He turned and then it hit me: it was YenaBoy45721 from the hotel. He recognized me and his ears went up. "I didn't know you were a private charter pilot."

"Yes." Wait, who pays thousands of dollars for a private charter flight to New York, but stays at a mid-priced resort in the Caribbean, not on the beach? If you can afford a plane trip like this, you can afford a fancy hotel room.

"Wow! I'm so glad to see you again," he said, ears up and perked. "One thing, this isn't too much luggage, is it?" he asked, pointing to his suitcases. There are two heavy duty packer crates, a rolling suitcase, and two briefcases. It's a lot of luggage for a single person, but it was not unwieldy. The G280 seats nine, plus their luggage.

"Not at all. I should let you know our flight attendant took sick last night with awful food poisoning. We're not going to be able to provide that service on today's flight. She might be better this afternoon, but last I talked to her, she was going to a local hospital."

"That's sounds awful," he said, surprised. "Do we need to wait for her?"

I shook my head. "I don't think it's getting better anytime soon. I made sure she's taken care of."

He smiled and I caught his tail wag a little. "That's good of you. You really are the captain of this plane."

I puffed out my chest. "Thank you," I said. "Here, let me help with the luggage. Then we'll have you on your way."

ဆ

The climb out of Guadeloupe went smooth with minimal turbulence. We leveled off at 41,000 feet and later went up to 43,000 feet as we cleared the Lesser Antilles. From there, it was just blue sky above with the ocean and clouds below, straight on until the U.S. east coast. Only Bermuda was out there, a distant and small set of islands off our intended flight path.

"Did you want to check on our passenger?" Donovan asked me.

"I thought you said you were going to do it."

"You're the captain. It gives you a chance to stretch anyway."

I wanted to protest, but curiosity about who Charles Danforth was kept me from ordering him back there. I was also feeling slightly nauseous for some reason. Still, I wasn't going to let him think he was in control here. "You sure? I don't mind watching the instruments," I offered.

"Not at all," he replied quickly.

He called my bluff, and I was either going to have to order him back there or agree to his suggestion. "Fine," I said, getting up and climbing out of the captain's chair. The plane was on autopilot anyway, and there wasn't anything to do except watch the instruments.

I slipped behind the curtain partition and entered the passenger part of the plane, passing the small kitchenette in the front across from the cabin door. Mr. Danforth sat at one of the tables in the front of the cabin with a laptop and some manila folders out. He seemed to be going over some paperwork.

I coughed to get his attention. "Again, I have to apologize for the lack of a flight attendant. We've left the Lesser Antilles and are now over the Atlantic. We're in the part of the flight where only one pilot is needed. Can I get you something to drink?"

The hyena looked up at me. "Do you have any coffee?"

"I can make some," I said, going over to the kitchenette. It's an exquisitely set up bar with a sink. The coffee maker is built in below and I pulled out the carafe and filled it from the sink. "Do you have a preference on the coffee? We've got a dark Guatemalan roast, a French roast, and a flavored hazelnut roast."

"Oh, uh, let's do the French roast."

I nodded, opened the packet, dumped it in, added the water, and set the machine to brew. I glanced around. I knew Bettie Jane used a small serving tray, but I had no idea where that was stored. "I believe you said you liked cheese on your menu preferences?"

"You guys read that?"

I leaned down and pulled out the cheese platter from the fridge we picked up in the morning. "Yes." When I stood back up, my head swam a little, and I stopped for a moment, surprised at the sensation. Maybe I needed to get my ears checked. I never felt like this.

"Oh, I'm still getting used to flying charter and the fact I don't have to go through TSA."

I shook my head to clear it, and I walked over, putting the cheese plate on the table away from his files. "If I might inquire, what made you decide to take a private charter this time?"

"Work."

"I see." That would explain the large luggage totes. He said last night he did medical research and development, but the paper he had pulled out looked like some type of engineering diagram with a strange arc detailed. "What is that?"

He looked up at me. "This is my life's work. It's a bionic tail designed to integrate with an amputee's remaining nerves while giving a natural look. It will revolutionize the prosthetic business."

This was breakthrough research. I couldn't think of what to say. Chuck was totally out of my league, but the coffee maker beeped then. "Your coffee is done," I said, going to pour him a cup. "I'll let you do your work. Just shout if you need one of us."

His ears lowered. "You don't want to stay and talk?"

"You look busy."

He picked up the files and started putting them back into his briefcase. "No, no, you're fine. I was just getting a jump on my work for when I return home. Please, sit down."

I sat down as he put his work away, and then looked at me, ears forward, focused on me. "I get really engrossed in this. I founded the company two years ago and we're working toward commercialization, and it's been a big rush to finish this and get it to market," he said to me.

"It must be very profitable, if you are traveling via charter."

"Not yet. Right now, these aren't for sale on the open market. It's still a lot of work to fit someone, they have to get a surgical implant into their nerves, and the mechanics are costly. We're working toward bringing the price down. The tech is so revolutionary though, it's going to change everything. It's not just tails we're working on, but that's been an untapped market and we're pioneering those first. There's been a lot of interest in what we're developing, although we've had to put security measures in place to keep competitors from stealing our research."

"I gather all the luggage is equipment for your work then."

"Yeah. I've got a prototype along with some specialized tools to do nerve mapping. It's cheaper to fly charter then replace the equipment if it gets damaged. We've got a client down here we're fitting for one. I have some adjustments to make with the biomechanics interface, but the results have been amazing! We're finally bridging the gap between flesh and machine."

Wow, was he smart. Just thinking about this was making my head spin. I felt so dumb suddenly for some reason. I wanted to just giggle. "All this is your work?"

"It's a team project. I developed the electrode graft and connection, hence why I do the test fittings. One of my employees specializes in the fur matching. One specializes in the mechanics. Et cetera. I've got a team of twenty. There are some scientists in China working on biologically grown fur that would really make this better, but we're using a synthetic nylon product right now." He paused and looked me over. "I'm rambling a little, aren't I?"

"This is all a little over my head," I admitted. The headache I had wasn't helping either.

Chuck laughed, flicking his tail against the chair. "Sorry, it's been my life's work. My doctoral thesis was about this. I'm super stoked to finally have helped push this forward and toward commercialization. I get a little carried away about it sometimes."

"That does sound like a good life's work," I said. "I just fly planes."

"That's fun, isn't it?"

"I enjoy it, but traveling all the time gets tiring."

"I can see that." Chuck picked up a piece of cheese from the platter and popped it into his muzzle. "Oh, this one is really creamy."

"They said they're an assortment. There should be some Queso De Papa, Munster, Brie, and one I don't remember the name of."

"This sounds really good. Did you want some? I don't want to eat this whole plate by myself."

"Thank you," I said, and reached for a piece of cheese. "I don't know what all these taste like."

"Neither do I," he laughed, "But we'll make do somehow."

I popped the piece of cheese into my mouth. "Huh, this one is kind of too ripe."

"Let me try." He picked up one of those and tried it. "Wow, that's a little bit of an acquired taste."

"Yeah, I don't like it that salty either." What was it with everything tasting salty to me today anyway?

"If it's too ripe, I just don't find it tasty," Chuck said.

I grinned goofily. "Hey, as a fox, if I can keep my natural musk in check, so can the cheese."

He grinned and leaned forward. "Even naked and aroused, you smelt better than the cheese."

My ears snapped back, surprised, but a part of me was really amused by this. "I don't know if I have a response to that." At least not one that I could do on the job.

"That's probably a bit far," he said, turning away.

I reached out and put my hand on his. "It's okay. You have a strong musk too, and I liked the scent of it."

His ears reddened. "I uh… um…"

I glanced toward the curtain separating the flight deck and got a wild idea in my head. A moment of perverse inspiration I couldn't let go of came to me. It popped out in a way that even though my pilot training told me it was wrong, I suddenly didn't think it mattered. I leaned over the table close to him. "Want to do something forbidden?" I whispered.

His ears perked, but he leaned forward. "What?"

I got up from the table and started walking to the back of the plane. "Come with me."

He followed me to into the washroom after I opened the door. Unlike a commercial airliner, the bathroom in the G280 is actually a decent size that goes across the entire fuselage and includes a vanity with a mirror on one side and a toilet on the other. There is even a window in the bathroom, a touch you don't see on commercial jetliners.

I pushed him up against the back wall of the bathroom. "If we're quick, my first officer won't notice," I whispered. Not like Donovan would care.

At first, he wanted to protest, but then he grinned. "Yeah?"

I undid his belt. "Yes, but we have to be quick."

He winked, and I pulled down his pants and underwear. Already he was semi hard. I nuzzled his sheath and was quickly greeted by something harder. I took him into my muzzle and made quick bobbing motions, holding his cock in my hand to keep him steady. I suddenly really needed this.

He went fully erect on me in twenty seconds. Chuck was excited, and I could feel his tail flicking against the bulkhead.

"Hey, watch it," he whispered to me when I got a little too eager. "No damaging the goods."

I realized I was playing with the tip too much, so I deep throated him, taking him all in, before coming up for air and working him with some quick strokes. My head was spinning a little, but I got a good rhythm going before he started to moan and his shaft twitched in my muzzle. This time, when he came, I did my best to make sure to catch every drop before I broke off.

"Did you want me to blow you?" he asked.

"No, let me get back up front before—"

The door to the bathroom opened. "All right, time to break this up," came Donovan's voice. I turned, expected to see him furious, but instead, he looked calm and collected. He also had a pistol in one hand and a self-defense stun gun in the other. I froze then, with my hand around the hyena's dick, a dribble of cum falling to the carpet.

Chuck looked up and growled at Donovan, his eyes narrowing. "What is the meaning of this?"

"I want what you develop."

I had my hand on the hyena's rapidly flagging dick, my muzzle had the taste of hyena jizz in it, and there was a tiger pointing a gun at me. "Donovan—"

"Shut up!" he hissed and motioned for me to move away from Chuck. "You keep quiet, and you'll get out this alive, Jonas."

The hyena looked down at me, and then up at the tiger. "Who do you work for?"

"Myself. Now if you want to get off this plane alive, you are going to do exactly what I say."

I felt the plane start to bank, the autopilot obviously following a preprogrammed course. "Where are you taking us?"

"The Bahamas," he said, "but that won't matter. By the time the authorities figure it out and find you, I'll be gone. Now where is the tail prototype?" he asked.

The hyena squared his shoulders. "It is in the luggage compartment. You can't get that till we land."

The tiger smiled. "On the contrary, the G280 has an access hatch to the luggage compartment from the passenger area. You just had sex against it."

I saw Chuck feel the gap in the polished wood bulkhead he leaned against in an oh-shit moment. "You realize this research could benefit a lot of people. Natural looking and acting prosthetic tails are going to revolutionize the medical field and restore expression abilities to hundreds of thousands suffering from tail loss or nerve damage."

"I know," the tiger said, "and they could be worth billions. That's exactly why some people want the tech you've been developing, and they think it's cheaper to steal it than license it. I'm just helping facilitate the business deal. Now, if you would be so kind, Mr. Danforth, I'm going to need you to sit down for the rest of the flight."

The plane had completed its turn and levelled out again. The hyena went to pick up his pants. "You can leave those. Getting you two to hook up is the most exciting part of this plan. It's worked out even better than I expected."

"Getting?" Chuck said.

"Yeah. I figured seeing each other available looking for tail at the hotel might provide a useful distraction for me. I wasn't sure foxy boy here would go for it, but just turning on Barked on his phone and providing some encouragement was all it took."

I growled at him. "You set us up?" I stood up, and the whole room suddenly spun, and I had to hold onto the back wall.

"Last night was all you. Today was mostly you."

Mostly me? I did just blow a passenger on my plane, but I… I would never do that. Why did I just do that? "What?"

He smiled. "I was worried I might get the dosing wrong, but apparently, I nailed it."

"If only Bettie Jane was here."

He chuckled. "I took care of that problem last night. She'll be fine by tomorrow. I just needed her off the flight. Now, Mr. Danforth?" said Donovan, stepping back into the passenger compartment.

The hyena glanced at me. "What did you do to Jonas?"

"I just slipped him a little GHB. Enough to make him easier to control." The tiger waved the gun. "Come on now. Jonas, you stay in the bathroom for the moment."

The hyena walked out of the bathroom and then stopped. "You know what I think of you?" asked Chuck, when he got close.

"What?" said the tiger, keeping the gun leveled at him.

"I think you're sick."

"If you want, the Bahamian authorities can ship you back to The States in a body bag. It's your choice."

This asshole was going to hijack my plane!

Chuck turned away, returning back to his seat. "Here is fine?"

Donovan followed him. "Yes, now I want you to—"

I'd had enough of this shit. No one was hijacking my plane. Even under the influence of the drug, I was not going to let someone steal my plane! While he had my back turned to me, I crept forward.

"Hey! Stay back there—" Donovan said, turning around, sensing me coming forward.

I'm still not sure if was impaired judgement or real bravado, but I leapt at the tiger, a hundred and forty pounds of angry swift fox, not thinking that Donovan was easily over two hundred. He was quick too, but he didn't bring the gun up to meet me. Instead, he pushed the stun gun into my chest.

I managed to get in a good punch in before the uncontrolled spasming of my body from the electricity coursing through me knocked me to the side. Chuck sprung up trying to pull the gun away from Donovan, and I could hear the electric discharge of the stun gun while I laid there in the aisle trying to breathe. The world felt like it was spinning.

They struggled, and in the confrontation, I saw the pistol get kicked down the aisle of the plane toward the bathroom. I had to push myself up, gasping to get my breathing under control, before I dove for the gun and came up with it in my paws.

"Stop!" I screamed, pointing the gun at the two.

Donovan had the hyena in a headlock and was trying to shock him. "Put that down, or he's toast."

I snarled. "Let him go!"

"You know that's only loaded with blanks," sneered the tiger.

"It is?" I said confused.

He nodded and kept the chokehold on Chuck. "Put it down."

"You're lying."

"I can't… breathe!" screamed Chuck, as he was shocked.

"Put the gun down," said the tiger, "or I'm going to finish him off now."

I didn't know how to handle a weapon like this, and I couldn't expect my aim to be good. My head still felt stuffed with cotton. In a split-second decision, I decided to do something crazy. I lowered the gun. "Blanks you say?"

"Blanks," he said, dumping the wheezing hyena into the seat and stepping toward me, blocking me from the cockpit.

"Then let's see if that's true," I said, pointing the gun at one of the windows and pulling the trigger.

The roar of the gun was deafening in the cabin of the plane, but it was immediately overtaken by the sound of rushing air. The bullet blew out the window, and I was jerked into the chair next to the broken window as the cabin depressurized. The gun fell out of my hands and slid away from me before the autopilot could correct for the sudden change in aerodynamics. Immediately the cabin pressure alarm sounded from the cockpit, and oxygen masks dropped from the ceiling.

Explosive decompression on an airplane is not a fun experience for anyone involved. At 43,000 feet, you have ten to fifteen seconds of useful consciousness before hypoxia sets in due to the thin external atmospheric pressure. If you don't grab an oxygen mask in that time, you'll become euphoric and then black out from lack of oxygen in the blood stream. Standard procedure is for a pilot to grab their mask, attach it, make sure your co-pilot has their mask on, and immediately begin an emergency descent to 10,000 ft. Then you call out your mayday, once you have the situation under control.

Being next to the hole in the plane made it difficult for me to grab the mask, and I had to flail wildly at the flapping contraption before I was able to grasp it and slip my muzzle into the yellow mask cone and gasp for air. The roar of the engines and the wind hitting the hole at Mach 0.8 was deafening. I held on, feeling my fur ripple in the wind, heart wildly pounding.

I stood up slowly, feeling unstable. I took a deep breath, fighting the wind, and then moved forward into the next row of seats and where Chuck was in the chair on the opposite side. I shoved my muzzle into the yellow cone next to his seat, and then took stock of my situation. Wind still whipped through the cabin, but the turbulence was less severe here.

Chuck had managed to grab a mask, and was looking at me, panicked. Up front, I saw Donovan had tried to reach the plane's controls and had collapsed in the doorway to the flight deck. He was slumped against the entrance frame, clutching the cockpit curtain.

"What do we do?" came the panicked call from the hyena, as he pulled off his mask briefly.

"Just wait," I called back. "The autopilot is going to bring us down lower." I could feel the plane already descending to a safe altitude, the Automatic Emergency Descent System having engaged when no one had tried to override the autopilot. It was there in case we failed to respond to an incident to bring a stricken airliner down to a safe altitude where crew could be revived. Without input, it would descend to 10,000 feet and hold that in the hopes someone could resume control.

I waited, clutching an oxygen mask, ears pinned back against the wind, trying to gauge our altitude against the clouds and featureless ocean below. It takes about five minutes to drop the 33,000 feet in an emergency like this. The system would do that as fast as possible without going over speed, but it was still a waiting game. In my hazy state, it felt like forever.

After a while, I could feel the plane starting to level off, and I pulled the mask off my muzzle.

"You okay?" I yelled at Chuck.

"I think so," he said, ears pinned back due to the roar in the cabin.

I noticed that in the seat in front of him sat Donovan's flight bag. It was unzipped, and I went through it. There was some rope and duct tape in there, so I took a piece of rope out. "Help me secure Donovan," I said, walking over to the collapsed tiger. He was passed out, but it looked like he was breathing shallowly.

"Is he okay?"

"I don't know, and I don't care right now," I yelled over the wind, pulling Donovan's arms in front of him and starting to loop rope around him. "We tie him up, and then I'm diverting to the nearest airport."

"Right," Chuck said, helping me secure Donovan. Once we had his arms tied, we dragged the tiger into a seat and looped rope around him to try and keep him in place. Then I used the duct tape to keep the rope secure.

Against the bulkhead, I found the stun gun, which I picked up and handed to Chuck. "If he wakes up and tries to start shit, shock him."

"Yeah, no problem. I'll keep an eye on him."

"Good." I stepped onto the flight deck and climbed into the captain's seat, putting the headset on, and checking our position. We were out in the middle of the Atlantic, heading away from Bermuda toward the eastern Bahamas. I wasn't sure exactly where Donovan was planning to take the plane, but Bermuda was still the closest destination. My heart was pounding and my head hurt like the dickens. I wasn't in any condition to fly, but I had no choice.

I turned the radio to 121.5 MHz. We were pretty far out, but Bermuda should still be within range. "Mayday mayday mayday, yankee-foxtrot-six-six-niner, one one zero miles south of Bermuda, requesting emergency landing," I called into the headset, letting my training kick in.

The response came back immediately. "Bermuda approach calling Yankee-foxtrot-six-six-niner, what's your emergency?"

"Bermuda approach, this is six-six-niner," I said, starting to bank the plane towards Bermuda. "We had an attempted hijacking and decompression incident. Aircraft is secure, but requesting approach vector and landing."

For a moment there was nothing. "Six-six-niner, say again?"

"We had an attempted hijacking and decompression incident, requesting emergency landing at Bermuda International."

"Roger six-six-niner. Turn left heading zero-two-five, altitude at or above ten thousand if able."

"Turn left zero-two-five, maintain ten thousand, six-six-niner," I replied, and then sighed to myself silently. I was so going to get fired for this.

⚓

Mr. Charles Danforth was whisked away by the police after we arrived, to have his statement taken. I went to the hospital, got blood taken, and ended up sitting with an IV in a hospital room until they thought my body had purged enough of the drug to be released. Then a parade of people came and asked me questions. The police who interviewed me in Bermuda found the whole thing kind of funny. The civil aviation authorities who I saw next had a scowl on their muzzles. Dispatch, however, was raging angry when I finally was able to call them. Bettie Jane, when I spoke to her that night after all the dust had settled, was just mildly amused.

"Wow, you hit the mile-high club finally," she said when I was done with my story.

"That's never been a goal of mine," I said into my phone inside the small hotel room the police arranged for me. It was cheap, it was uncomfortable, but it wasn't a prison cell. I was pacing trying to relax, my tail whipping behind me in agitation.

"And you stopped an attempted hijacking."

"I'm pretty sure they're going to can me."

"For what? Providing excellent customer service beyond the expected standards of the airline?"

"Bettie, really? I almost got everyone on that flight killed. I had a serious lapse of judgment."

She chuckled. "You got drugged, Jonas, but you still got everyone on that flight on the ground safely with minimal damage to the aircraft."

"I guess."

"No, seriously. You kept your head even though you were under the influence."

"That doesn't mean they're not going to fire me."

"Shh. It will be okay. Just let yourself rest, okay? You saved the day. It could have been a lot worse. You didn't even crash the plane."

My ears fell. "I had sex on the job…"

"It's going to be the only time you ever get to do it too," she laughed. "Where do they have you anyway?"

"I'm in a hotel room. The nurses didn't think it was worth keeping me, but I have an appointment mid-morning with a doctor."

"See, they didn't even lock you up. You'll be fine. I fly back to New York tomorrow, but they haven't given me a new assignment yet. Have they booked you home yet?"

"Not yet. They're still investigating things here. It will probably be a few days before they let me return. I know the police want to talk to me again."

"Well, when they do, let me know okay? We should do lunch or dinner. Just not with Donovan. That guy's a creep."

"I don't know what they're going to do with him, but I imagine he's going to be in jail for a while."

"Oh yeah. This one is definitely a story."

"You sound upbeat at least about it."

"I spent over twelve hours throwing up. It kind of puts things in perspective."

"I can imagine," I sighed into the phone. "You going to be okay?"

"Yeah, the doctors said I'll be fine, but I'll get myself checked out again now that we know it was some type of drug. Let me call the hospital up."

"Sounds good," I said.

"Have a good night, Jonas, and keep your muzzle up. I'll talk to dispatch and corporate in the morning about how they need to keep you on. You've got good reflexes."

"Thanks, you have a good night too, Bettie Jane, and let me know what the doctor says," I replied, hanging up the call. I sank down onto the bed, letting myself feel the weight of the day. I sighed and stared at the ceiling. Maybe I could just sleep this off. Was it too early to go to bed?

I picked up the phone and squinted at it. The time said 9:47 PM, and I had a message on Barked. That hadn't been there when I called up Bettie Jane.

Concerned, I swiped down to see who was poking me now. It was from YenaBoy45721, and it read, *I'm sorry about what happened today. They finally let me go, but I'm stuck in Bermuda while the investigation proceeds. The company lawyer is hella mad at me, but the prototype I tested down in Guadeloupe is secure, so that's good. Perhaps we can meet for breakfast tomorrow?*

I scowled. I wasn't sure we should be seeing each other right now, so I typed out, *You sure you want to?*

The response was simple. *Uh, you seem nice? You're my hero at 40,000 feet?*

That gave me a chuckle. *Thanks, but I'm not sure that means I'm going to keep my job.*

The response was simple. *Oh shit! I'm so sorry, it's all my fault.*

I glanced at where my phone said YenaBoy45721 was located. It said approximately 1,500 feet, so obviously a different hotel in the downtown area, but not far. *Nah. You're not the one who slipped me something on the plane, and I'm the one who took up the offer from the cute stranger at the hotel bar. There were some strings, but I'm kind of glad I did. It's quite a story, so if you give me directions to a breakfast place, we can meet.* I pondered for a minute and then hit send on my message. I was already in deep anyway, what was I going to lose now?

Great, I'll look for a place and let you know. I know nothing about Bermuda, came back the response.

Cool. Chuck did seem like a nice guy, thoughtful, and considerate. I wasn't sure where this was going, but I always wanted a guy like this.

I rolled over on the bed, listening to it creak. This thing was awful. I was so tired, but I was still hyped up from earlier. I picked up my phone and pondered for a minute. *You know, I could go for some company tonight. It's lonely in here. Just not at my place this time. The bed here sucks.* I typed into the phone and sent the message.

Sure! But sex is the furthest thing from my mind right now, came the response a few minutes later.

That's fine, no pressure. I just don't want to be alone right now. There was something about what I just went through that itched at the back of my mind.

Yeah, me either, Chuck sent back. *I'm tired, but I don't know if I can sleep.*

I knew that feeling for sure. *Yeah same,* I sent. I wanted more than anything to wrap some spotted fur around myself and just doze off. I smiled and got up from the uncomfortable bed. At least one thing today had worked out.

I had for years wanted to write a vampire story before I wrote Loving You is Wrong. *Appearing on my Patreon in 2019, this appeared on* The Voice of Dog *podcast in 2020, and the story won a 2020 Leo Literary Award. The shortest story in the collection, I'm working on writing a full treatment of Ekrem and Radic that explores their relationship more.*

Loving You is Wrong

"Is it time yet, Radic?" you ask as I tire, having spent the last few hours poring over old manuscripts you got for me. I can only smile and beckon you to me, Ekrem. Somehow your timing is always perfect, and your warm fur against my body entices me in ways you can only guess at. Everything about this is wrong, and yet we both do this dance willingly.

I know my touch is cold against you, but you never complain. You never shrink away, and I know not if I have enthralled you, or if it is you who has enthralled me. I no longer care, honestly. A fox like myself could easily feel inferior with a leopard like you, but you don't shrink away from me. You take me by the hand and lead me to the bed. You welcome me inside of you with grace and love. It makes me feel alive again as I watch you getting on top of the mattress and then beckoning me.

With you lying there on the sheets, I want everything you will give me, and everything you won't give me. The blood in your body is warm, and it calls to me. I lick my fangs hungrily. I should care, but I am hungry. Hungry for you. So hungry for you it hurts. I want to drink you in until there would be nothing left. I worry someday I may. I worry about that a lot.

I climb on top of you, and your legs lift. Your tail lashes in anticipation and your shaft gets hard. I smile, whispering sweet words to you. "Now it is," I say, and you shiver. You shiver every time. I thought it was magic the first dozen times, but I have put no spell on you. It is you who has put a spell on me. I hate you for that too, and yet I would want it no other way.

The lube is always right on hand too, as I look for it. I know you put it away, so you planned this. You read me so well. It is in that moment, as I feel myself hardening, my knot starting to grow as I slick myself up, that I wonder why you love me. Why do you stay with me? Even down there, I am cold, but you never mention it. It must feel strange when I enter you, my dear Ekrem, and yet you do not complain. Instead, you beckon me. You wrap your arms around me, as I line myself up. Your raspy tongue licks at the scruff of my neck. Most would run away from a monster like me. You instead submit.

As I thrust inside, you writhe under me in ecstasy. Each push drives you further toward the edge. Your spotted fur bucking against my red and white body. You cry out in pleasure, your claws digging into my fur as you have to hold on. I just want to ravish you, each thrust driving me crazy. Each moment giving me a little bit of your warmth that I so desperately hunger for. The fact it is so brief makes me curse the gods that created this world, but if this is all that's left that I can get from life, it will be enough.

You moan out in pleasure, and even my breathless voice rasps while we intertwine. Your eyes squeeze shut in ecstasy. Your heart beats so loud, I can hear it pounding in my ears. The blood that keeps you alive taunts me, just below your skin. Each of my thrusts make it whisper a seductive song in my ears, and yet… it's not that which I want in these moments. It is to see you happy that drives me, to see you satisfied, and every time you are, after I have spent myself inside of you.

Later, as I snuggle up to you on the bed, my mouth grazes your neck, and I have to resist the urge to bite and taste that coppery delight. It would be easy, so quick to take it all, and yet I would never forgive myself. I would never be happy again. It's tough being happy when you're me, so instead I get close and let the scents in your fur envelop me. Even after sex, you smell like earth, leaves, and sunlight. It reminds me of everything I've lost and can only experience through you. My soul, if I still have one, longs for these things, and yet with you, I have them again. I have everything a fox could desire. It's why I worry so much about losing you.

My leopard lover, I am wrong for you, and yet I am with you. I love you, even if it's wrong. I have wondered if I should bind you with my embrace, but I do not wish you to suffer like I have, Ekrem. I do not wish you to ever feel the way I do, a cold body that does not breathe with a heart that does not beat. You don't complain, though. Why don't you complain, Ekrem?

I know time is against us also. I shall outlive you and someday you will be gone and I will still be here, in this world, alone again in this castle. I need only drink all of you, and then give you a little of myself to bind you to me forever, and yet… I haven't. I can't curse you like I was. I know sometimes you beg me to do it, to bind us forever, and I am beginning to realize I will. But not today. Not yet. Not while you're still warm against me in this bed. Not while I still have time to look for a cure to see if I can free myself of this curse.

"Do you need to drink, Radic?" you say, as we're lying entwined together, my tail draped over your hips.

"No," I lie. I am hungry, but I wish to see no harm come to you, Ekrem. I wish to see no harm come to anyone. I will again hunt in the dark just before dawn and attack some cattle down in the village. It will keep me going, even if it's not potent enough to satisfy me.

The warm blood in your body taunts me, it tempts me, but I will hate every moment of it when I finally drain you. I will take no pleasure in it, if that is the only way we can live. An eternity in death together is still a pale shade of life. I miss the sun, and as I curl up against you, I can feel the hints of it still on your fur.

As long as we can stay here, as long as we can be together, I think I still have a soul. I do not believe vampires still have souls, but somehow with you, I do. With you, Ekrem, I still am alive.

Silk and Sword *was published by FurPlanet in 2010 in*
FANG Volume 9. *It is the prequel to my novel* Scars of
the Golden Dancer. *Set three years before the novel, this*
story deals with prostitution and is the starting point for
Zayn's journey.

Silk and Sword

The silk is smooth in my paws, its dark lustrous nature beautiful, its allure appealing, and its shame upon me unmistakable.

"I thought you would want something appropriate for tomorrow."

I look up at Usman. The cheetah's expression is apprehensive, and I know why. Men do not wear silk; it is taboo. "It's beautiful," I whisper, trying to keep my emotions in check.

"I hope it fits right. My wife got the fabric from Hafiz last month. He said the silk would go well with your fur coloration. Farida cut and tailored it just for you."

I look down at the fabric. Holding it in my hands, the dark green silk contrasts well against my sandy fur. To wear this will mark me as less than a man, but is that not what I am becoming?

"Zayn?"

I look up at Usman again. We are standing in his market stall in the caravanserai, tucked in the back under the arch of the nook it occupies, away from the bright light of the courtyard beyond. Ceramic cooking vessels and plates are stacked up around us along with a couple of sun-bleached carpets tucked against the back wall. A collection of iron cooking utensils sits out front on a rug along with some colorful plates that catch the sun outside. It's a setting I know well, but today it feels different.

"Sorry, just admiring her work. Thank you," I manage to get out.

The cheetah wrings his hands together. "Do you want to try it on?" he asks me cautiously.

I gulp and nod. "Yes."

"Then let's go somewhere private," Usman suggests.

We jackals have a proverb we tell our children: opportunity, like a good meal, does not last. Both my parents were fond of this saying, and those words have been on my mind a lot during the last month. This is a great opportunity for me, and also the crux of my descent.

We have retreated to an alcove inside the caravanserai where goods are stored. A half dozen large, clay, water storage jars sit on one side while some baskets are stacked on the other. By shimmying between them to the back of the alcove, there is some privacy behind the baskets where they obscure the view from the main hallway. Only a little mid-day light filters in through the high-cut windows, but even here in the shadows, I know I can't hide my shame.

The dark green fabric, with bits of emerald green thread interwoven into it, is soft against my golden pelt. I would not have thought it a good match, but wearing it I realize why Hafiz selected it. Even in the low light of the alcove it shimmers.

The cut of the skirt is excellent. It drapes off my hips while leaving the front open and my tail free. I must give Usman's wife, Farida, credit for this. Her craftsmanship is impeccable. She has even sewn a line of small beads on the hem and provided fabric for me to tuck under myself to cover my maleness. She has completed the look with a simple top that covers only my upper chest, leaving my stomach and arms exposed. The top is a little loose, but I'm sure I can have her adjust it. Included in the clothes is a scarf of sheer dark blue fabric to dance with.

Of course, all her expert work still doesn't change what is happening to me and instead reinforces it. Now that I'm wearing this, my manhood is truly gone. My father died by the sword out in the desert, cut down by raiders. I am to be pierced by a different kind of sword.

"Well?" asks the cheetah.

"Farida does good work," I offer.

"She does, and Hafiz was spot on about the fabric. You look very striking in that."

My ears fall back. I know why Hafiz knew the fabric would look good on me. He regularly comes to sell here, and I've caught him staring at my tail before as I go about my odd jobs. He knows what I am becoming. The fact I fit this new position in life so well concerns me. Have I always been destined to do this?

"Zayn," says the cheetah, obviously picking up on my hesitant feelings, "you don't have to go down this path. We'll think of something else for you."

I close my eyes. "I can't keep borrowing money from you, Usman. I still don't know how I can repay you for this."

"Don't worry about that. The cut of your earnings is enough."

"Right." On top of his normal work as a trader, Usman arranges the dances, and each dancer pays a small bit of their purse to him. I will do the same, just like the other girls. From his fee he pays the musicians and earns a few coins for himself.

He sighs softly. "You've been practicing your footwork, like I suggested?"

"Yes, Usman," I say, with a bob of my head. For the last two months, whenever they do the dances, I follow along on the roof of the caravanserai, letting myself twist and twirl through the darkness of the night just like the dancers in the courtyard below, trying to fix the beats in my head while the girls earn their keep.

He nods and runs a clawed hand through the fur on top of his head. "Then tomorrow, I will debut you. I have clients willing to pay good coin for one of your proclivities."

I nod and start taking the outfit off. I don't want to be reminded of my shame right now.

"Zayn?"

I stop and look up. "Yes?" The skirt falls to the ground, but I resist the urge to pick it up. I need to get comfortable being exposed now.

He wrings his hands. "Your father would be proud of you. Both your parents would be actually."

"What?" I glare at Usman and then gesture down. "Proud of this? Of me?"

He looks away from my nudity. "Yes," says the cheetah. "You're stronger than anyone else I know. It takes courage to do this, especially for a man. One does not simply lie there and take it without suffering the scars of their profession. Your father was a survivor, no matter where the rains fell. You have to be here in Zaptu. He always kept his ears up for trades to make and goods to transport. He didn't go down in that raid without first taking a number of the attackers with him. Few would notice, but I see that same steel within you."

I don't feel any steel inside myself right now. I feel only the crushing sensation of what I'm undertaking. My mind wants to cry out in panic, but I am holding it down. Maybe that is my strength in this. "Thank you."

The cheetah claps a hand on my shoulder. "I try and make sure all my dancers earn good coin. I will do my best to make sure you do as well, so you can retain your family honor."

I nod, and he walks off then, leaving me to take the top of the silk costume off in private. Slowly I pull it off and carefully fold it up.

Since Hafiz chose the fabric I'll be wearing, I can only hope that means he is looking to buy my attentions for the night. He knows what I'm going through. He has always treated me well, and I know he shares my proclivities. I'd like my first night to have some meaning. Amare, a wolf a few years older than me, has told me about his times with Hafiz, so perhaps tomorrow I'll finally get the chance to experience it firsthand.

That hope helps stills some of the dread inside of me.

I remember when I was young and my parents' house had furniture in it. My father worked hard as a trader and caravan master. Like most homes here, it's made of mudbrick, but its two small rooms are comfortable. We had wall to wall carpets, wooden chests to keep our cookware and clothes in, and a divan. My parents even had a bed, but when father died, my mother slowly had to sell off the furniture to make sure we could eat. When she died, I sold the rest of it. Now the two rooms are empty save for one carpet, my sleeping mat, and a chest that is too battered to fetch much money.

Before me is a small plate of dates, the only food I could afford in the market today. These dates are overripe and past their prime, but I used all the coin I had left to buy them. Odd jobs around Zaptu are hard to come by, and I owe the Emir taxes. It's only a few dirham, but if I don't pay soon, he will lock me up and give my home to someone else. Usman can't afford to employ me as an apprentice, and while he has been able to kick me some work, I cannot rely on that.

My father's sword and one of my mother's shawls sit on the carpet across from me. These are the last personal effects of my parents I still own. Next to them, the silk outfit is also sitting on the carpet, waiting for me. A small clay bottle of olive oil sits on top. I'll need that once my client for the night pays for my attentions.

I pick up a date and chew on it, letting the sweetness play across my tongue. There is a sourness underneath the sugar, but these will give me the energy I need for tonight. I've already brushed out my tail, but I couldn't afford a bath today. Water is scarce on the edge of the dunes, so the bath I took two weeks ago will have to do.

There comes a knocking that pulls me out of my thoughts. Getting up, I go and unbolt the worn wooden door. "Yes?" I say, swinging it open, letting the bright light of day flood over me. Outside is a jackal with a pelt darker than my own.

"Oh good, I was hoping to catch you at home, Zayn."

"Hafiz! I did not expect you to come by." We exchange formal cheek kisses. "Come in, come in! My home is your home."

"Thank you," he responds, and when I gesture to the carpet, he goes and sits down.

"Would you like a date?" I offer, reaching down and lifting up the plate. Even though it is all the food I have, it is customary to share my meal. Even in my growing poverty, let no one say a guest in my home was mistreated.

"Just one," he responds, taking a date and tossing it into his muzzle. He cringes as the taste hits, but he swallows. "Thank you."

"Things go well?" I inquire, walking over to the chest to pull out my battered kettle. "I can brew tea."

He holds up a hand. "There is no need. I wasn't planning to stay long." He gestures to a spot across from him, so I can join him on the rug. "I need to get back and help pack up my stall. I have my two assistants already doing that."

"You are leaving?" I say, surprised, as I sit across from him. He generally makes the three-day journey south to Zaptu once a month to sell for a week. He only came into town two days ago.

"Tomorrow. Sales are slow, and while two caravans just came into town, they don't trade in cloth. I'll return north and see how things are going back home. I'll be back through next month."

"Well, that is sad news, but you are coming to see me dance tonight?"

He flicks his ears. "You are doing it tonight?"

I wave my paw over to the silk. "Usman gave me the outfit yesterday. I've been practicing,"

"Farida is quite the seamstress, I hear."

"And you have quite an eye for color. It matches my fur well."

The other jackal smiles. "Excellent," he remarks, "I look forward to tonight then."

My tail wags. At least my first customer will be someone I care for. "I can show you a preview, if you wish."

"Oh no. I'm happy to wait till tonight. Plus, I don't want to disturb your preparation."

"Sure," I say, with a little regret. I forget to keep my ears up.

"Oh, don't be so disappointed," chuckles the other jackal. "You need to be focused on tonight. This is your big moment. I did want you to know, though, I'm not going to be through this area much anymore."

"Why not?"

"Trade has been shifting south, and most of the caravans are heading straight for the Sultanate of Khalin. Plus, the local Emir has raised his taxes to compensate for a lack of income.

My trip next month may be the last trip I make in a while. Unless things change, I'm not going to stay and sell."

The markets in the city of Aksu are said to overfill with goods, enriching the Sultan who rules on the other side of the mountains.

"You'll need to go to Khena to buy fabric, won't you?"

"Only for the silk and cotton I can't get locally. I'm considering making a trip to Aksu next year to buy cloth. I sit on too much of the high-priced stuff now."

"Ah," is all I can say.

"But tonight is your night. I can't wait to see it." He leans forward to give me a cheek kiss. "I will see you later."

"Of course, Hafiz."

He gets up, and I lead him to the door to let him go. I watch from my doorway as the other jackal strides out into the bright light of day, heading back to the caravanserai that dominates this small town. I guess I should finish getting ready for this evening. Tonight with Hafiz will be bitter-sweet, but this is my life now.

❧

I leave home just before the sun touches the horizon. It is still hot out, but it will quickly cool once the sun sets. I have the silks wrapped up in a bundle of cloth I carry under one arm. At my hip, I have my father's sword, its presence reassuring. The eyes of my neighbors flit over me, but do not linger. No one says hello either, and that surprises me.

Zaptu is a small village of mud brick homes clustered around the stone walls of the caravanserai. Nestled in a little valley among the foothills, the entire town spills out from the caravanserai's main gate. To the west lie the mountains and to the east the great sands stretch out to the horizon and beyond. Trade is the lifeblood of our little town, otherwise this place would be little more than a well and a palm tree grove.

Life here is always hard. There are years it doesn't rain, years where the only grazing for sheep and camels is far away. The shepherds sometimes have to travel quite a distance to feed their herds on what little vegetation the dunes and hills can provide. Only by offering a good respite from the elements for those weary souls who reach our home are we able to survive out here.

The caravanserai is the center of life in our little town. A square stone structure with high walls, it shelters the travelers who pass through here. The interior of the building hosts a grand courtyard with nooks off it that traders can rent to sell their wares. Spread around the building are the baths, storerooms, and sleeping quarters that serve the weary. Our Emir also makes his home here, along with the treasury of the village. A single gate controls access to the fortress.

Once inside those stone walls, I run into Amare. He has set up a small stand to sell kebabs near the entrance where he is cooking over a camel dung fire. The wolf is bent over the coals, carefully tending the meat when I walk up, so I have to call to get his attention.

"Hey, how are sales tonight?"

He looks up at me and quickly glances down. "Good."

"I'm surprised you are in here," I say, coming around to the side to talk to him. "Are you moving over from the village square permanently?"

The wolf looks up at me and slowly stands up. "Zayn…" he says softly.

My ears splay in confusion. "Yes?"

He glances around. "We can't—" he stops to gulp, "we can't be seen together anymore. You know that, right?"

"What!" I say, shocked.

"With you taking up the dance, I don't want anyone asking questions they shouldn't." He bends back over the fire.

"Amare, we're friends," I hiss.

The wolf's ears flick at the sound of my voice. "Do you wish to buy a kebab?"

Is that it? Are we no longer friends? "Amare..."

"Do you wish to buy a kebab?" he repeats, not looking up at me.

I stand there gawking at the wolf. I have not yet stepped out wearing the silks, and already I am unclean? It can't be the act of sex with a male either that turns Amare away from me. I know what his heart desires, but to admit that in public is anathema?

I turn and slowly walk away into the crowd milling about the courtyard, the parcel carried under my arm. Glancing around, I can see familiar muzzles turn away when I meet their owner's eyes. I don't want to be here now if this is how I am to be treated. Already my shame is known, it seems. I am only to be an object to be desired, and no longer a presence to be acknowledged.

"Zayn!"

I stop. Usman is coming up to me through the crowd. He puts a hand on my shoulder as I turn to meet him. "Once they've finished lighting the lanterns, the crowd will begin assembling for the dances."

I want to speak, but my throat is tight, so I just nod.

Even though dusk is falling, my limp tail and stiff posture is unmistakable. "Are you going to be ready?" he asks.

"Usman, by doing this, am I unclean?"

He blinks and pulls his hand back. "Who said that?"

"Amare won't talk to me anymore."

The cheetah rolls his eyes. "Amare thinks no one knows what he does in the stable at night with the visiting camel drivers. I have heard stories."

"Yes, but... am I unclean now?"

He glances around. "I never said this would be easy. You know that," he says, so only I can hear him.

"That still doesn't answer my question."

"Because only you can answer that. Only you can feel the shame others might try and force upon you." He looks around the courtyard, and in that moment, the cheetah looks older. There is gray fur around his eyes and flecks of gray in his hands. "But no matter what they say, only you will feel the hunger in your belly," he adds.

And then I realize what I should have known before. Usman doesn't run the dances because he wants to see young woman sell themselves out. He runs the dances because he knows from experience what drives someone to this point. I have seen the way some of the older adults of our village treat Usman and give him a wide berth. I thought they had disagreements that dated to before I was born, but now I see it was more.

"You've done this yourself, haven't you?"

The cheetah nods.

"Why did you never tell me before?"

He tilts his head and chuckles. "Because you must make your own decisions. It was years ago also."

"And yet some remember, don't they? They still think you're less of a man."

He shrugs. "Some will never forget, but time heals many wounds." He stops to take in a breath. "Do you wish to still take up the mantle?"

I don't have to do this, but I can't expect Usman to support me either. He has a wife and two young kits now to feed. He's done all he can do for me without me doing something for myself.

I suck in my breath. "Yeah."

The lantern light is low, but I can see the other dancers getting ready as I pull the top over my head. The silk garment falls neatly around my shoulders, and I tie it into place. The fabric is velvety against my paw pads. It has a heavenly feeling to it, a far cry from the rough wool and cotton I normally wear. I check the skirt to make sure it is lying right. My maleness is covered by the fabric, but its presence can still be seen in the bulge it produces. I close my eyes for a moment, just letting this sink in. It's too late now to turn back.

A good dancer can earn up to four or five silver dirham a night if they're lucky, although two or three is common. The dancers usually perform twice a week at the caravanserai, although many do private engagements. Work follows the rhythms of the caravans, and tonight we have two new ones in town. It looks like we'll have a good crowd, so everyone should get a buyer for the night.

"Do you have your routine down?" one of the other dancers asks me.

I open my eyes and look at who addressed me. A jackal named Nawra is standing before me. She has red silk draped from her hips, and a heavy, silver necklace hanging from her throat along with silver bracelets at her wrists. Her breasts are left exposed.

"Yes. I've been practicing it as often as I can."

"Good. Now don't focus on any one person too long. The more you flirt, the more tips you'll get. You never know who might want to bid either." She points to the sword on top of my clothes. "Are you doing a sword dance?"

A sword dance is dangerous. Dancers have been known to cut themselves on their own blades. "I hadn't thought about that, but I could try. I brought it more for moral support."

She shakes her head. "If you have not practiced it, do not attempt it. Later, after you've danced a few times, I can teach you how to do that."

"Thanks," I mumble, as she looks me over.

"Do a quick twirl for me," says Nawra.

I oblige her and perform a twirl.

"Good, but you need to watch how you let your tail flow." She demonstrates for me. Her tail neatly whips around behind her as she turns. "Now you try it."

I repeat the motion for her.

"Again," she barks, "and be mindful of your tail."

I do it again, trying to keep my tail from flying everywhere.

"Better. You'll need to work on that, but it will do for the moment. Good form can earn you some extra coin."

"I'll try and keep that in mind. I'm kind of nervous about tonight."

She smiles. "Usman will make sure you earn well."

It's more than just the dirhams, at least for tonight. Next time, it will just be for the coin. "I think I know who will bid on me tonight."

She quirks an ear at me. "Don't ever count on that. You earn your keep by pleasing the whole crowd, not one person."

"You have your admirers, don't you?"

She shakes her head and claps a paw on my shoulder. "I haven't earned as much silver as I have by being anyone's favorite. Sure, some will take a liking to you and come back, but it's never a sure thing. Every good whore knows that if you ever fall in love with one of them, they'll end up breaking your heart."

My ears fall. I know Hafiz will only be here for tonight, but surely some of the girls have stable clients.

"It's a tough lesson to learn," adds Nawra. "It took me a while myself, but do not despair. We look out for each other, and that will include you, Zayn."

I don't know Nawra that well, so I just nod. She lets go of me, and before I can dwell on her words, Usman comes in to make sure we're ready. He collects our personal effects for safekeeping, and we wait inside the caravanserai for his return so we can begin the night's festivities.

When he comes back, we exit the building in a procession to yips and growls from a raucous audience happy to see us. The nine of us take seats on cushions next to the musicians beside the small area that serves as the stage. They place me in the center of the group, signifying that I'll be in the middle of tonight's program.

As I'm taking my seat, I see Hafiz in the audience, who smiles and waves to me. I flash him a smile back, and he bobs his head in response.

Usman steps forward and gives a short spiel to the prospective buyers. Then the first dancer, a lioness who has been doing this for a number of years, gets up, steps out, and begins her routine as the musicians start to play. The ney, with its soft whistling notes, and the oud, with its plucked strings, combine with the beating drums to create a tapestry that tickles the fur in my ears and entices the body to move.

When the lioness finishes, the bidding is quick and with a seductive flash of fangs from her, her attentions for the night have gone for three and a half silver dirham. The next dancer than steps up and takes her turn.

Nawra goes just before me. "Watch my tail," she advises, as she gets up and steps out in front of the audience, a set of zills in each of her hands.

Once the music starts, Nawra's movements are smooth and fluid, as the drums beat out a quick tune for her. She follows along with the zills, using the finger cymbals to accent her movements. She is graceful, her hips mesmerizing, and indeed Nawra does place her tail carefully as she moves, her spins and shimmies expertly executed. Her body responds to every note of the music, the drums driving her forward. The audience is enraptured by the thrust of her hips, and even I can appreciate the sensuality of her movements.

When she is done, she takes a bow, and Usman steps up to begin the bidding for her attentions. The calls are quick, and Nawra walks away with four silver dirham and three coppers to a caracal trader. He grins toothily at his prize as the money exchanges hands and then leads her away.

With Nawra's dance complete it is now my turn. I get up and smooth down my clothing before walking out carrying the sheer blue fabric Farida provided.

There are some hoots, but the crowd is quieter than it was for the other dancers. Still, I smile to the audience and bob my head respectfully, not looking up to meet anyone's eyes. My role is to be the receptive partner, so I don't want to look aggressive. It is time for me to offer my wares.

"And now for a treat we haven't had here in a while," calls Usman to the audience, "may I introduce our newest performer, Zayn."

There is muted applause and Usman steps back, leaving me alone in the middle of the circle. If I wanted to back out, it's truly too late now. The whole town can now see my new role. My heart beats fast, but I keep my body still, waiting. It feels like forever before the music starts.

Finally, I hear the first notes for the song I asked for, my song for tonight. I spring into action then, placing my feet as I have carefully planned out as the ney begins the song, followed by the drums.

At first, I feel stiff, my motions nervous. My footwork is sloppy, and I find myself out of sync with the drums. I have to pivot faster than I intended to catch up, and that leaves me with more momentum than normal. A second correction, and I drop back in sync, getting the carefully practiced stomach roll right.

Slowly I'm able to loosen up. Having watched the other dancers up close, I'm aware how much better I could be. I can only hope that my hips, stomach, and rear cover up some of my missteps and offer something alluring to these men that they haven't had a chance to bid on in a while. I do my best also to control my tail, just like Nawra suggested, but I can tell I will need to practice these motions later.

At one point, while doing a hip motion with my left side, I catch Hafiz watching me in the audience. Eye contact is brief though, and it's impossible to keep my focus on him. I also remember I'm supposed to please the whole crowd, so I let my gaze wander through the audience.

Near the end, I have my steps in sync with the drums and ney, and I finish on a high note. I take a quick bow as people clap. It sounds like I've won over some doubters with the response I get. I pant and wag my tail; I've done it, and now it is time to bid for my attentions. In that break, I glance over to Hafiz again who smiles, still clapping. Usman steps up and nods to me before he turns to the audience. "An excellent first dance! Now, who would like Zayn's attention tonight?"

There is a murmur. It has been quite a while since a male has performed here, so I don't know what to expect.

"Half a dirham," calls out a voice I don't know.

"Half to start. Do I hear three quarters?" responds Usman.

I look toward Hafiz, who smiles back at me. He hasn't placed his bid yet.

"Three quarters!"

"A full silver!" retorts the first voice.

This is good, but I hope they won't try and outbid Hafiz. I glance around to see who is trying to buy my attentions.

"Excellent," says Usman. "Anyone else?"

There is a murmur of voices from the crowd, but no on one else speaks up.

"A silver dirham going once! Going twice!"

Why hasn't Hafiz bid? I glance back toward the jackal, but I can see him talking to someone now.

"A silver dirham it is then," calls Usman, the cheetah rests a paw on my shoulder. "Good luck, Zayn," he says softer, just to me, as he pulls out from under his kaftan the small bottle of olive oil he's holding for me.

"Thanks," I whisper. I turn and walk to the side. I can see a leopard coming over to me. Through the crowd, I glance toward Hafiz, but the other jackal is gone. He never planned to buy my attentions, did he? My heart falls at the thought.

"One silver dirham," says the leopard, holding up two half dirham coins, now that he is within earshot. I don't know who he is, but I think he's one of the merchants who came to town today. This isn't who I was supposed to be with tonight. This isn't who I wanted to be with tonight.

"Yes, sir," I manage to get out. I hold out my hand for the money, trying not to let it shake. He drops the coins into my palm, and I quickly pocket the coins into a pouch in my dancing outfit where I've tucked the bottle of olive oil. I try and smile to welcome my customer. "And where shall I entertain you this evening?"

The leopard grins. "Come. I've rented a room here tonight that will be comfortable. I trust you can provide all services?"

"Of course, from now until dawn."

The leopard smiles, a smirk creeping onto his muzzle. "Excellent." He turns. "Come then, let us take our leave."

Dazed, I follow him into the inside of the caravanserai. As I walk away from the crowd, I glance back toward Usman. He's just introduced the next dancer and is stepping back. I will have to ask him tomorrow how he came to do this. I want to look for Hafiz, but I have to keep up with the leopard. My time for the rest of the night is no longer my own.

We enter the building and he turns toward where the rooms rented to travelers are. I follow the leopard down the hall, my mind racing, trying to make sense of what just happened. Did my dance displease Hafiz? Did I go for more money than he expected? Surely, he must have known I'd command at least a silver dirham. Many of the other dancers go for much more.

In my dazed reverie we turn a corner, and I'm forced to look up. There is Hafiz, talking to one of his assistants in the corridor. I let out a soft bark and stop dead in my tracks.

The other jackal looks up, then quickly turns back to his assistant, and keeps talking louder than before about some wool he sold earlier in the day. I step forward and stop. His ears twitch, but he does not glance my way.

The leopard turns to me, having gone a few steps further. "You aren't going to keep me waiting, are you?" he asks, tapping a foot.

"Coming," I say through gritted teeth, walking past Hafiz. The other jackal doesn't look at me as I pass, and each step is like a stab in my heart. In my new role, like Amare, he will not associate with me now.

Down the hall the leopard stops and takes out a key to unlock his room. As he opens the door to his rented quarters, my blood pounds in my ears. He takes a lantern hanging against the wall in the hall and lights it before he ushers me into the room. Then he hangs the lantern on an iron hook before he closes the door behind us.

"Undress and get on the bed."

I gulp. This is it. This is who I've become. This is what I do now for a living.

"Yes, sir," I whisper, slipping the silk off, after taking out the small clay jar of olive oil. I let the silk fall to the ground, and I force a seductive smile. As I get on the bed, I can hear a low contented rumble from my client. I do not care what his name is, I just hope that he will be gentle.

About the Author

NightEyes DaySpring is a known troublemaker who is rumored to have a penchant for coffee and an interest in dead, ancient civilizations. He has been writing furry fiction for over twenty years. His stories have appeared in various anthologies, including *Werewolves vs. Fascism*, *Heat*, and *FANG*. Currently, he resides in Florida with his boyfriend where in his spare time he masquerades as an IT professional, plays board games, and doodles.

Visit his website, *nighteyes-dayspring.com*, for more about his writing. For day-to-day nonsense, follow @wolfwithcoffee on Twitter.

www.ingramcontent.com/pod-product-compliance
Lightning Source LLC
Chambersburg PA
CBHW070938190726
48292CB00004B/1238